PAGES OF DESTINY

WHISPERS OF THE VOID

LCB

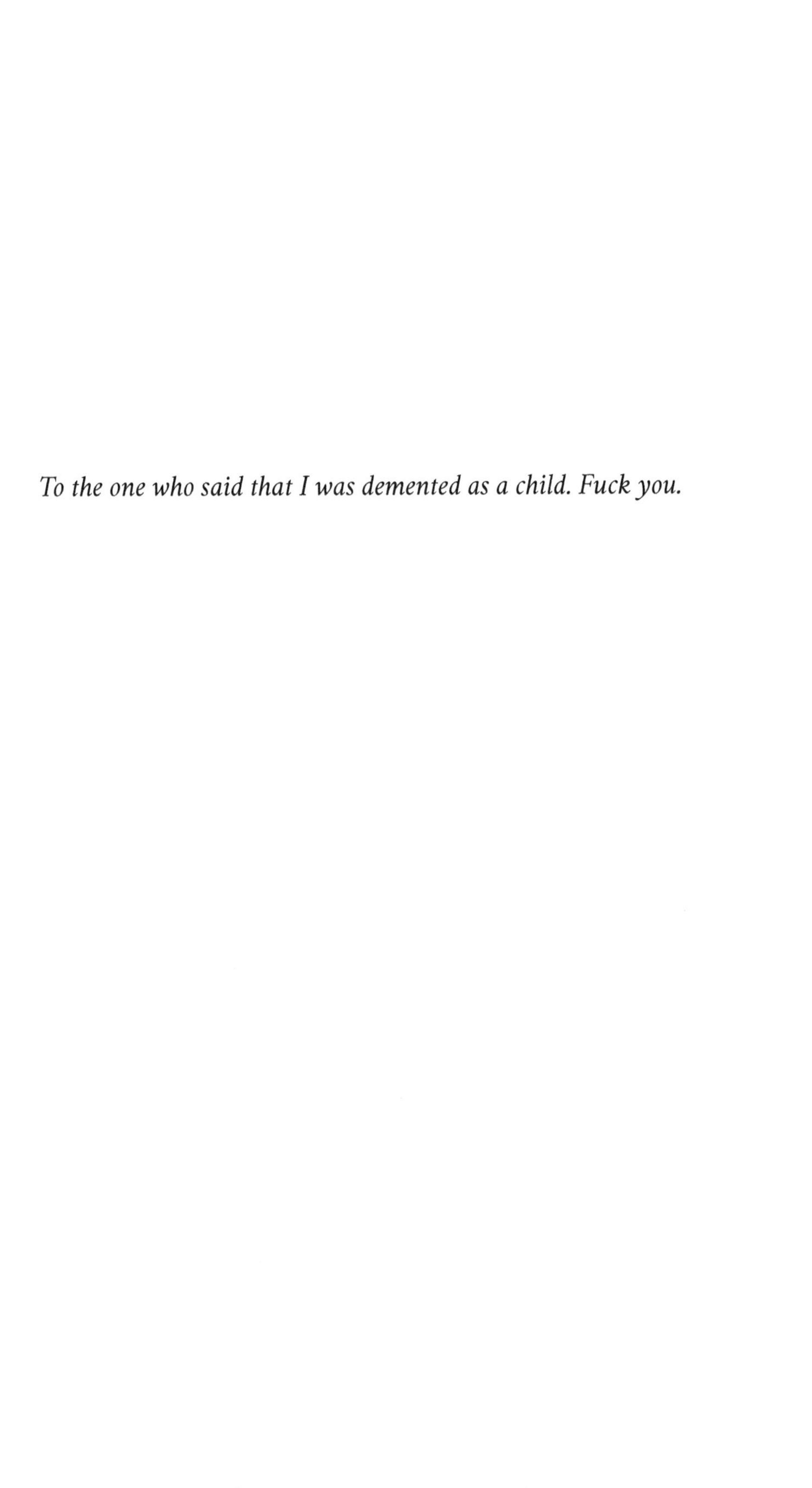

To the one who said that I was demented as a child. Fuck you.

Aetheria
RAVENSHO
NIGHTSHA
FORTRE
ECLIPSE
CITADEL
DUSKVEIL MOUNT
VALORA
CASTLE
VOID GAT
SHADOWMIRE FOREST
VALCORA

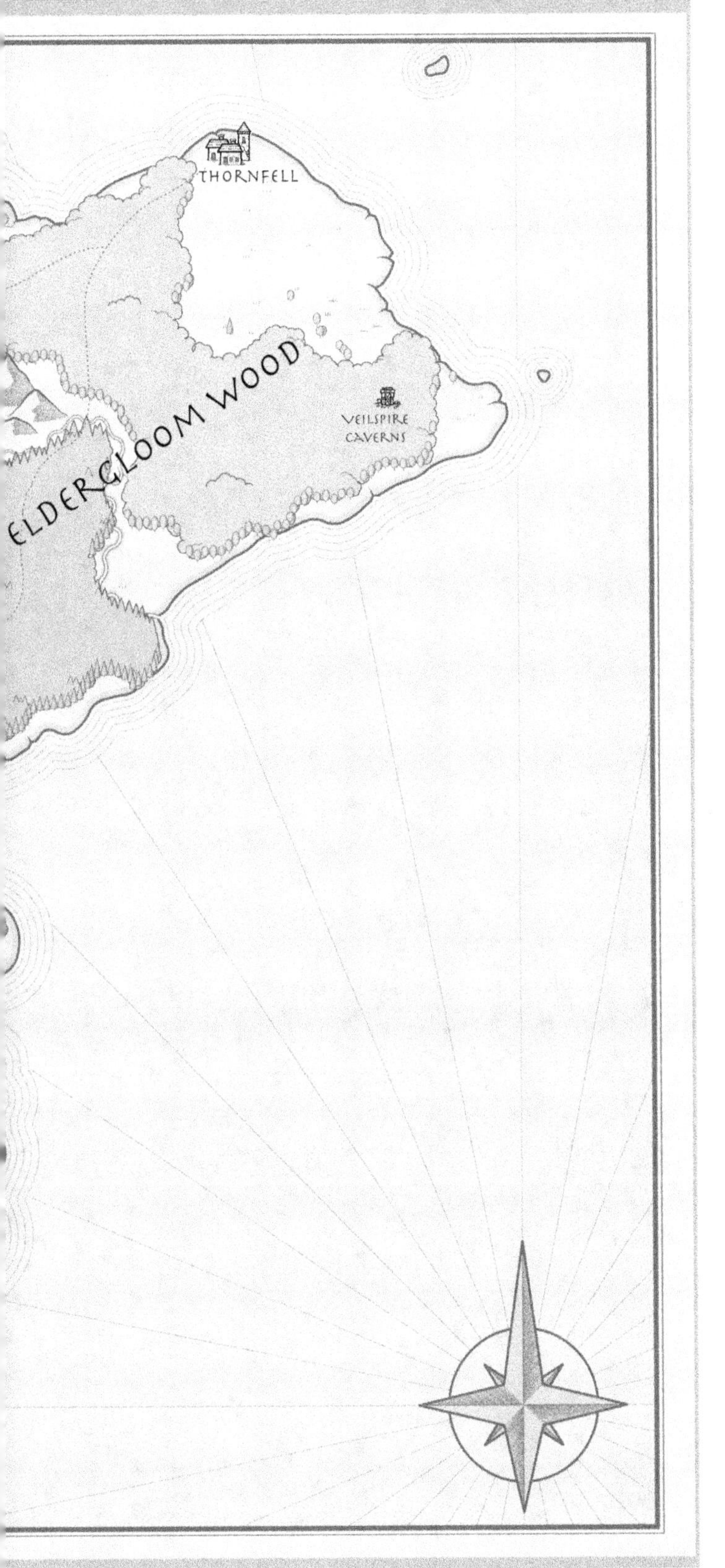

THORNFELL
VEILSPIRE
CAVERNS
ELDER GLOOM WOOD

CONTENTS

PROLOGUE

In a quaint village nestled amidst ancient forests and rolling hills, lived a reclusive young woman named Eudora Wisp. Known for her eccentric ways and captivating blue eyes that seemed to hold secrets of ages past, Eudora spent her days secluded in a cozy cottage surrounded by shelves upon shelves of old books and curious artifacts.

One stormy evening, while the rain drummed against the windowpanes and the wind whispered eerie melodies through the trees, Eudora found herself inspired like never before. Her quill danced across parchment as she penned words that seemed to flow from an otherworldly source. The ink shimmered with a faint, ethereal glow, as if infused with magic itself.

Unbeknownst to Eudora, each stroke of her pen bound

the pages of her book with spells of ancient power. The story she crafted spoke of a distant realm called Aetheria, a land of swirling mists and enchanted forests, where mythical creatures roamed freely and magic thrived in every leaf and stone.

As Eudora completed the final chapter of her tale, the words on the page began to pulse with a soft, inviting light. Curious and drawn by an inexplicable force, she touched the quill to the book's cover, whispering the title she had chosen: "Chronicles of Aetheria."

In an instant, the room was engulfed in a dazzling whirl of colors, and Eudora found herself standing in a lush meadow under a sky ablaze with unfamiliar constellations. Before her stretched a path lined with shimmering crystals, leading deeper into the heart of Aetheria.

In this new world, Eudora discovered that her book was more than just a story—it was a gateway to a realm where her words held the power to shape reality. She met characters from her tale who welcomed her as a revered storyteller, guiding her through lands of wonder and danger alike.

Yet, as Eudora delved deeper into Aetheria, she realized that her book had also attracted darker forces—ancient evils and jealous beings who sought to possess her creation for their own ends. With each chapter she wrote, the balance of magic in Aetheria shifted, echoing the turmoil within Eudora's own heart as she grappled with the consequences of her newfound power.

Driven by a desire to protect both worlds, Eudora

embarked on a quest to restore harmony to Aetheria and safeguard the magical book that had brought her there. Eudora Wisp, known now as the Weaver of Tales, returned to her homeland with the enchanted tome in tow. Using magic she acquired in Aetheria, Eudora established the Whispering Wisp Bookstore and concealed the mystical book among its shelves, patiently awaiting the destined individual who would help set things right.

CHAPTER ONE

A GRAY, UNEVENTFUL DAY

In the heart of a bustling metropolis where skyscrapers brushed against the clouds and neon lights painted the night sky, lived a young woman with an insatiable curiosity for the world beyond her office cubicle. Her name was Brea, and like many, she had once been drawn to the allure of corporate success. Yet, as the years went by, she found her days blending into a monotonous routine, each one a faded echo of the last. The fluorescent lights of her office seemed to cast a permanent shadow over her ambitions, dimming her once-bright dreams.

On this particularly gray and uneventful day, Brea sat in her cubicle watching the clock, waiting for the last five minutes of her workday to tick away. She leaned back in her chair, sighed, and absentmindedly tapped her fingers on her desk. The youthful excitement she once felt about this life had long since withered. Now, all that remained was a quiet longing for something more.

Finally, the moment she had been waiting for arrived. With the click of a button, she clocked out and hurriedly gathered her things. The rain outside had picked up since the morning, a relentless downpour that seemed to mirror the storm swirling inside her mind. She stepped into the elevator, her thoughts preoccupied with how little the life she'd built resembled the one she'd dreamed of.

As soon as the doors opened into the lobby, Brea rushed outside, her umbrella barely withstanding the fierce gusts of wind that whipped through the city. The streets were crowded with people, all as eager as she was to escape the rain, but the downpour made it hard to see beyond a few feet. The sidewalks were becoming flooded, and Brea, already soaked from the wind's cruel angles, knew she wasn't going to make it home dry.

A small, warm light flickered in her peripheral vision—a bookstore café. It was tucked away between two towering buildings, as though hidden from the world unless you knew exactly where to look. Desperate for shelter, Brea darted toward it, barely managing to push open the creaky door before the wind tore her umbrella from her grasp.

The soft chime of a bell announced her arrival, and the scene before her was a stark contrast to the chaos outside. The bookstore was a world frozen in time, its shelves lined with ancient books and the air filled with the earthy scent of old paper. Dim, warm lighting gave the space an almost magical ambiance, and the rich aroma of freshly brewed coffee mixed with the comforting smell of worn leather and aged parchment.

"Goodness me, look who's wandered into my humble shop!" A voice called out from behind a small cafe counter. "Haven't seen a fresh face in here in ages. What brings you to my little sanctuary of books, dear?"

Startled, Brea turned to face the speaker. Behind the counter stood an elderly woman with dark silver hair pulled back into a neat bun, her wrinkled hands clasped together. She seemed very old, as though she could have been there since the store was first built, but her eyes gleamed with a young, mischievous light.

"Oh, hi!" Brea replied, a bit embarrassed. "I couldn't resist the charm of your bookstore… and the fact that it's pouring outside."

"Yes, the storm's a fierce one today, isn't it? My shop's a good place to wait it out." The woman smiled warmly. "Care for a cup of coffee? You're looking a tad cold, dear."

Brea hesitated. The old woman seemed friendly enough, and the bookstore had a certain charm she couldn't quite explain. She nodded and allowed herself to relax, hugging her arms around her damp clothes as she moved further into the shop.

The rain continued to hammer against the windows, but inside, the world was quiet and still, as if the outside chaos didn't dare intrude on this peaceful sanctuary. The old woman, strange as she was, felt like a gentle presence, her shop a place where time itself had slowed to allow weary souls like Brea to catch their breath.

With a sigh, Brea settled deeper into the coziness of the shop, unaware that her life was about to take a turn far beyond anything she could have imagined.

CHAPTER TWO

THE WHISPERING WISP

Brea's eyes wandered over the shelves of books surrounding her, each one unique in size, color, and texture. But one, in particular, caught her eye—a book bound in weathered leather, adorned with intricate gold filigree that shimmered faintly even in the dim light. It stood out from the rest, almost as though it was waiting for her to notice it.

Intrigued, Brea made her way to the shelf. She reached out, her fingers brushing the cover gently. The moment her skin touched the leather, a strange sensation rippled through her—warmth, tingling, almost like a soft current of energy. Startled, she pulled her hand back, but her curiosity got the better of her. She gingerly took the book down from the shelf and flipped it open.

The pages glowed with a soft, ethereal light. The text was

written in an elegant, flowing script in a language she had never seen before. Yet, as her eyes traced the unfamiliar letters, the words seemed to come alive on the page, pulsating with a rhythm that synced with her heartbeat. A strange, almost magnetic pull drew her deeper into the book's mystery.

Brea gasped, dropping the book as if it had burned her. It hit the floor with a soft thud, and she quickly looked around to see if the old woman had noticed. She was relieved to find that Eudora, as the nameplate on the counter read, was still busy behind the café counter, seemingly unaware of Brea's fumbling.

Brea bent down to retrieve the book, but as she straightened up, she found herself face-to-face with Eudora and let out a surprised squeak. The old woman held a steaming mug of coffee in her hands, a small smile tugging at the corners of her lips.

"A little jumpy, aren't we, dear?" Eudora chuckled softly. She bent over with surprising agility for someone her age and picked up the fallen book, handing it back to Brea. "This one's special," she added, her tone cryptic. "It finds those who are meant to read it."

Brea flushed, embarrassed by her reaction. She took the book from Eudora's hands and smiled awkwardly. "It's just the weather, I think. Makes everything feel a little… strange."

"Perhaps," Eudora said, her gaze lingering on the book for a moment longer before she handed Brea the mug of coffee. "Or perhaps it's more than that."

Brea took a sip of the coffee, its warmth soothing her frazzled nerves. "This place is… lovely," she said, eager to steer the conversation back to something more normal. "I work just up the street, and I've never seen it before. It's like it just appeared out of nowhere."

Eudora smiled mysteriously. "The Whispering Wisp has a way of revealing itself when it's needed."

Brea wasn't quite sure how to respond to that, so she simply nodded and sat down in a worn leather chair by the fire. Eudora wandered off into the back of the store, leaving Brea alone with her thoughts—and the book.

CHAPTER THREE

A MYSTERIOUS BOOK

She couldn't resist. She picked the book back up, studying its cover more closely. The gold filigree swirled across the leather like the branches of an ancient tree, and the pages seemed to shimmer faintly with their own light. Despite the strange energy she had felt earlier, something about the book drew her in, as if it held secrets waiting to be unlocked.

Brea opened the book once more, tracing her fingers lightly over the glowing text. As she did, a sudden gust of wind swept through the room, though there were no windows open, no doors ajar. The fire flickered, and the air around her seemed to hum with energy.

Before she could react, the wind intensified, swirling around her like a vortex. The pages of the book fluttered wildly, glowing brighter and brighter until they were nearly blinding. Brea's heart raced as she felt herself being lifted from her chair, the world around her spinning and distorting.

And then, just as suddenly as it had started, the wind stopped. Brea was no longer in the bookstore.

She found herself standing in the middle of a vast, ancient forest. Towering trees stretched high above her, their leaves glowing softly in the fading light of three suns that hung low on the horizon. The air was thick with the scent of earth and moss, and the distant sounds of unknown creatures echoed through the trees.

Brea blinked, her mind struggling to catch up with what had just happened. This had to be a dream—a vivid, impossible dream. She turned in a slow circle, trying to make sense of her surroundings, but the reality of the situation was undeniable.

She wasn't in the Whispering Wisp anymore. She wasn't even sure she was on Earth.

"Welcome," came a soft, melodic voice from somewhere behind her.

Brea spun around, her heart leaping into her throat. Standing before her was a figure cloaked in shadow, their features hidden beneath a hood. Yet their presence felt familiar, like an old story she had once heard but couldn't quite remember.

"You have much to learn, traveler," the figure said, their

voice carrying an air of ancient wisdom. "The book has brought you here for a reason."

Brea's breath caught in her chest. "Where am I?"

The figure smiled beneath their hood, though Brea couldn't see their face. "You are in Aetheria," they said softly. "And your journey has only just begun."

CHAPTER FOUR

THE VOICE OF AETHERIA

Brea stood frozen, her mind whirling as she tried to make sense of what was happening. Aetheria? She had never heard of such a place. Everything about her surroundings felt surreal—the golden light of the three suns, the shimmering leaves on the towering trees, and the shadowed figure before her whose very presence made her heart pound.

"Why am I here?" Brea asked, her voice barely a whisper.

The figure's hooded face remained hidden, but their voice was soothing, almost hypnotic. "The book chose you, Brea. It has a way of finding those who seek answers, those who are ready for the truth."

"The truth? How do you know my name?" she questioned, feeling her confusion deepen. "I don't understand. This is a mistake… I was just at a bookstore, and now…" She trailed off, her words feeling hollow in the vastness of the strange forest.

The figure stepped closer, their footsteps silent on the soft forest floor. "There are no mistakes, only paths we do not yet see. The book brought you to Aetheria for a reason, traveler. You must find what it seeks to show you."

Brea's breath came shallow as the weight of their words sank in. This couldn't be real, she thought. She had to be dreaming, or maybe she'd fallen asleep in the chair at the Whispering Wisp. Any minute now, she'd wake up to find the fire crackling, the old bookstore comforting her with its worn, familiar atmosphere.

But as she glanced around, everything about this place felt too vivid, too real to be a dream. She could feel the slight chill in the air, smell the rich scent of moss and pine, hear the distant calls of creatures that roamed just beyond her sight. The figure, though shadowed, exuded a presence that was tangible and undeniable.

The figure gestured toward a path that seemed to appear out of nowhere, a narrow trail winding through the thick forest. "You must follow the path," they said softly. "It will lead you to what you seek."

Brea hesitated, looking down the trail that seemed to stretch endlessly into the unknown. "What is it that I'm supposed to find?" she asked, her voice trembling.

The figure did not answer directly. Instead, they raised a hand, and the book—the same weathered leather tome that had brought her here—appeared once more in their grasp.

They held it out to her, the golden filigree gleaming softly in the fading light of the suns.

"You will understand in time," the figure said. "The answers you seek lie within these pages, but the journey must be taken with an open heart and mind. Aetheria is a land of mysteries, but it also holds the truth of your soul."

"My soul?" Brea echoed, feeling as though the ground beneath her was slipping away. The weight of the book felt heavy in her hands as she accepted it from the figure. "I don't even know who you are."

The figure's hood dipped slightly, as if they were smiling beneath the shadow. "I am only a guide, a whisper on the wind. But you will come to know me, as you will come to know yourself."

With that, the figure began to fade, dissolving into the shadows of the forest. Brea reached out instinctively, but there was nothing to grasp. The figure was gone, leaving her alone with the softly glowing book and the path ahead.

For a long moment, Brea stood in silence, gripping the book tightly against her chest. She wanted nothing more than to wake up from this bizarre dream, to be back in her small apartment, warm and dry, with the sound of rain pattering outside her window. But the reality of Aetheria pressed against her, urging her to accept that this was no dream.

Her eyes fell on the path again, its narrow trail winding into the dense forest, disappearing into the unknown. She had no idea what waited for her at the end of that trail—or even if there was an end. But deep down, something inside her stirred. An inexplicable pull, like a forgotten memory rising to the surface.

With a deep breath, Brea tightened her grip on the book and began walking. Hopefully following this trail would lead to some answers.

The forest around her was eerily quiet, save for the occasional rustle of leaves overhead. The trees seemed alive, their branches arching gracefully above her like an ancient canopy, their leaves shimmering with an otherworldly light. Brea couldn't shake the feeling that they were watching her, observing her every move. She could have sworn she'd seen several of the trees move out of the corner of her eye, like they were following the trail with her.

As she continued down the path, the air grew cooler, the light from the suns dimming even more as if dusk was settling in. Strange shapes flitted at the edge of her vision—small creatures, perhaps—but whenever she turned to look, they vanished into the underbrush. A sense of unease crept into her chest. Were there dangerous creatures lurking in the shadows of the treeline, Brea would be sorely unprepared to defend herself. She had no weapons, nor any training for that matter. She had no idea how to fight something or someone off. Brea pushed these thoughts out of her mind and quickened her pace.

After what felt like hours of walking, the path opened into a clearing, and Brea stopped in her tracks. In the center of the clearing stood a towering tree, unlike any she had ever seen. Its bark was gold, gleaming in the dim light, and its branches twisted upward toward the sky, glowing softly. But what drew her attention most was the door carved into its trunk.

The door was intricately detailed, made of the same gold bark as the tree, with swirling symbols etched into its surface. It seemed to pulse faintly, as though it was alive.

Brea stepped closer, her heart pounding. She glanced down at the book in her hands, the glowing symbols on its pages now more familiar. They matched the carvings on the door.

She hesitated, feeling a mixture of fear and curiosity. The door was calling to her, just as the book had. Whatever lay beyond it, she knew it was the next step in her journey.

Taking a deep breath, Brea reached out and placed her hand on the door. The moment her fingers touched the cool surface, the symbols began to glow brighter, and with a soft creak, the door swung open on its own.

Beyond it was darkness—impenetrable, vast, and filled with the unknown. Brea thought about how ridiculous it would be for her to walk into that unknown, but realized she didn't have much of a choice. If she ever wanted to get home, she'd need an explanation as to how she arrived here in Aetheria in the first place.

Without another thought, Brea stepped through the doorway.

As the door closed behind her, the darkness enveloped her completely. But this time, she wasn't afraid. She felt the familiar pulse of the book in her hands, guiding her forward. The air was thick with magic, the kind that made her skin tingle and her heart race. Something about the book's presence soothed her nerves.

Suddenly, a soft light appeared in the distance, and Brea moved toward it. As she drew closer, she saw that the light came from another figure—this one different from the shadowed guide in the forest.

This figure was tall and luminous, with flowing robes made of light itself. Their face was serene, their eyes glowing with an ancient wisdom.

"Welcome, traveler. You must find the Heart of Aetheria," the figure said, their voice echoing softly in the stillness. "There, the truth will be revealed."

Brea's pulse quickened. Traveler. That's what the hooded guide had called her, too. "What truth?"

The figure's glowing eyes met hers. "The truth of who you are. The truth that the book has been waiting to show you."

And as they spoke, the book in Brea's hands began to glow brighter than ever before, the pages flipping open on their own. The symbols danced across the paper, rearranging themselves into words she could finally understand.

CHAPTER FIVE

WHISPERS OF AETHERIA

The air around Brea hummed with a palpable energy as the figure's words echoed in her mind: *The truth of who you are. The truth that the book has been waiting to show you.*

As the symbols on the pages of the book continued to shift and glow, Brea found herself transfixed by the sight. The letters, once incomprehensible, began to form coherent sentences. They glowed softly in the darkness, inviting her to read.

In the beginning, there was Aetheria, a realm where all truths converged, and all secrets were bound by the breath of the stars. And in Aetheria, there existed a Key—a being who could unlock the mysteries of this world and beyond. The Key was lost long ago, but the time has come for it to return.

Brea's heart skipped a beat as she read the words aloud to herself. A Key? The thought tugged at her mind, but before she could grasp it fully, the luminous figure beside her spoke again.

"You have been chosen, traveler," the figure said, their voice reverberating in the stillness. "You are the Key—the one destined to unlock the hidden truths of Aetheria. This realm has been waiting for you."

Brea's breath caught in her throat, her mind reeling. The Key? Her? The absurdity of it made her want to laugh, but the weight of the moment kept her grounded. This was no dream—no figment of her imagination. This was real, as real as the book she held in her hands and the strange, glowing figure that now watched her with patient eyes.

"I don't understand," Brea said, her voice trembling. "I'm no one special. I'm just... me. How can I be the Key to anything?"

The figure smiled gently, their luminous form radiating warmth. "You have always been more than you realize, Brea. Aetheria has called to you because it has sensed the power within you. But only you can choose to accept your destiny."

Brea swallowed hard, her mind whirling with questions. This mysterious figure knew her name as well. How did everyone she came across seem to already know her? More pressingly, she had never felt like someone who could hold any sort of power, let alone one that connected to an ancient realm like Aetheria. Her life had been ordinary—almost painfully so. And yet, standing here, she felt a pull deep within her, a longing to understand what it all meant.

The figure gestured toward the glowing pages of the book. "Aetheria has chosen you for a reason. This world is full of magic, secrets, and untold histories. But it is also a world on the brink of great change, and the Key—your power—can determine the fate of all who dwell here."

Brea felt her pulse quicken. "Great change?" she asked. "What kind of change?"

The figure's expression grew somber. "Aetheria exists in balance—between light and shadow, creation and destruction. But a darkness has been growing in the unseen corners of this realm, waiting for the moment to strike. You are the only one who can stop it. The Key is the only force strong enough to maintain the balance."

A chill ran down Brea's spine. She looked down at the book in her hands, its glowing text pulsating with an energy she was only just beginning to comprehend. Her fingers brushed the pages, and a familiar warmth spread through her, the same sensation she had felt when she first touched the book in the Whispering Wisp.

"I don't know if I can do this," Brea whispered. "I don't even know how."

"You will not be alone," the figure reassured her. "The book will guide you, as will others who understand the old ways of Aetheria. But your journey will not be without challenges. Darkness does not surrender easily."

Brea's mind raced as she weighed the enormity of what the figure was telling her. Aetheria needed her, but she had no idea where to even begin. How was she supposed to unlock the secrets of a world she didn't even know existed until a few hours ago?

Before she could voice her doubts, the figure extended their hand toward her, and a soft light began to glow in the distance—like a beacon in the vast darkness. "The first step of your journey lies there," the figure said. "Follow the light. It will lead you to the answers you seek."

Brea stared at the light, a mix of fear and anticipation swirling inside her. Every instinct in her body told her to turn back, to return to the familiar world she had known, where things made sense. But something stronger tugged at her, urging her forward. The book, the figure, the whispers of Aetheria—they had awakened something within her, something she couldn't ignore.

With a deep breath, she nodded. "I'll go," she said, her voice steadier than she felt. "I'll follow the light."

The figure smiled, a soft, approving expression. "You have taken your first step, Brea. Aetheria welcomes you."

The figure began to fade, their glowing form dissolving into the air like mist in the morning sun. As the darkness closed in once more, only the faint glow of the distant light remained to guide Brea forward.

Brea walked toward the light, her footsteps echoing softly in the vast silence. The terrain beneath her feet was strange, shifting between solid ground and a sensation of floating.

She felt weightless and heavy at the same time, as though she existed in both the physical and ethereal planes of Aetheria.

The light ahead of her began to grow brighter, and soon she found herself standing before a massive archway carved into a mountainside. The stone was smooth, covered in the same intricate symbols she had seen in the book and on the door of the great tree. The glow from the archway illuminated the surrounding area, casting long shadows over the ground.

Without hesitation, Brea stepped forward, passing through the archway and into the mountain. The air inside was cool, with a dampness that clung to her skin, and the steady sound of rushing water echoed through the cavernous space, making her feel small in the vastness of it. Shadows danced along the stone walls, flickering with the faint light that seeped through cracks in the ceiling, casting eerie patterns on the uneven ground. Every step she took seemed to echo back at her, making her acutely aware of how alone she was.

The narrow path wound deeper into the mountain, twisting and turning through the rock as if it were alive, guiding her forward with no clear destination in sight. Brea's heart pounded with anticipation and anxiety. The weight of the book in her hands seemed to pulse in rhythm with her steps.

As she ventured deeper, the temperature dropped, and the cool air became cold, biting at her skin. She wrapped her arms around herself, but the chill wasn't just physical—it felt as though something deeper was lurking in the shadows, something watching her every move. The path narrowed further, barely wide enough for her to pass, and the walls of the mountain pressed in on either side, as if the stone itself were trying to swallow her whole.

The sound of rushing water grew louder, and as Brea rounded a sharp corner, she found herself standing at the edge of a massive underground river. The water was dark, its surface rippling with a faint glow that illuminated the cavern in a ghostly light. A narrow stone bridge stretched across the river, leading to another tunnel on the far side. The bridge looked ancient, its stones worn and cracked with age, and Brea's heart tightened at the thought of crossing it.

She took a deep breath, steeling herself for what lay ahead, and stepped onto the bridge. The moment her foot touched the stone, the book pulsed sharply, sending a jolt of energy through her body. Brea gasped, stumbling slightly, and clutched the book to her chest. It was reacting to something—something powerful that lay ahead.

Each step across the bridge felt heavier, as if an invisible force was trying to push her back. The water below rushed faster, the glow on its surface flickering like the heartbeat of the mountain itself. She could feel the weight of the journey pressing down on her, the enormity of what she was about to face becoming clearer with every step.

Halfway across the bridge, the air grew colder still, and the faint light from the river began to dim. The shadows on the walls shifted, twisting unnaturally, and for a moment,

Brea thought she saw movement—something slithering just beyond the edge of the light. She froze, her breath catching in her throat. Her hand instinctively moved to her chest.

A low whisper filled the air, indistinct at first, like the wind passing through cracks in the stone. But as Brea stood there, her heart pounding, the whispers grew louder, forming words she couldn't quite understand. They came from the depths of the river, from the shadows on the walls, from the very stone beneath her feet.

"Turn back..." the voice whispered, soft yet filled with malice. "This is not your path..."

Brea's skin prickled with fear, but she forced herself to keep moving, her hand clutching the Book tighter. She wasn't going to let fear stop her now. She had come too far already. But with every step she took, the whispers grew louder, more insistent.

"You don't belong here..." the voice hissed, and Brea could feel a cold breath against the back of her neck, though when she turned, there was nothing there. "Leave, or you will be lost to the shadows..."

Brea quickened her pace, her heart racing as she neared the end of the bridge. The tunnel on the far side was just ahead, but it felt like miles away, the darkness stretching between her and her goal like an endless void. The whispers clawed at her mind, filling her with doubt, with fear, but she couldn't stop. She had to keep going.

Finally, she stepped off the bridge and into the tunnel, the cold air pressing in around her like a weight. The whispers faded, but the sense of unease remained. The path ahead was darker now, the light from the glowing river far behind her. The mountain seemed to grow quieter, the only sound the echo of her own footsteps and the faint, rhythmic pulse of the book in her hands.

The tunnel twisted and turned, leading her deeper into the mountain's core, and soon the ground beneath her feet became uneven, jagged rocks jutting up from the earth. Brea stumbled once, catching herself on the rough stone wall, her breath ragged from the effort of pushing forward. The air grew thinner, colder, and she could feel the magic in the mountain growing stronger, a presence that pressed against her mind like a living thing.

Suddenly, the tunnel opened into a vast cavern, its walls lined with ancient stone carvings that glowed faintly with an eerie, otherworldly light. The carvings depicted scenes of battle, of creatures of light and shadow locked in eternal conflict. At the center of the cavern stood a stone altar, its surface smooth and polished, and resting atop it was a small, glowing crystal that pulsed with the same energy as the book.

Brea's eyes widened as she stepped closer to the altar. The crystal's light flickered in time with the pulse of the Book, as if the two were connected, bound by some ancient magic. She could feel the power radiating from it, pulling her in, urging her to reach out and take it.

As she reached out to touch it, the sphere flickered, and an image appeared within its depths—an image of a vast city, shimmering under the light of multiple suns. The city was beautiful, yet something about it felt off, as though a shadow lurked beneath the surface.

Before she had time to comprehend what she was seeing, a figure emerged from the shadows at the edge of the cavern. Cloaked in darkness, their face obscured by a hood, the figure moved with an unsettling grace, their presence sending a shiver down Brea's spine.

"You've come far," the figure said, their voice low and smooth, like silk sliding over steel. "But you're not ready to face what lies ahead."

Brea's heart pounded as she stepped back from the altar, her hand instinctively reaching for the Book. "Who are you?"

The figure laughed softly, a sound that echoed through the cavern like the hiss of the wind through dead leaves. "I am a guardian of the path you walk. And if you wish to continue, you will have to prove yourself worthy."

Brea swallowed hard, her fingers tightening around the satchel. "What do I need to do?"

The figure's hood tilted, and beneath the shadows, Brea caught a glimpse of glowing eyes, burning with power. "You must face the darkness within you. Only then will you be able to control the Heart."

The words sent a chill through Brea's entire body. Face the darkness within? Control the Heart? The whispers from the bridge echoed in her mind, the voice of the mountain warning her to turn back. But she couldn't. She wouldn't. If the path ahead required her to face her fears, her doubts, her darkest self, then so be it.

"I'm ready," Brea said, her voice steadier than she felt.

The figure stepped closer, the shadows swirling around them like smoke. "We'll see."

And with a wave of their hand, the cavern plunged into complete darkness, swallowing Brea whole.

CHAPTER SIX

THE PATH OF SHADOWS

*B*rea awoke still in the cavern, lying on the cold stone floor. She stiffly stood to her feet and looked around her, searching for the figure from before. The figure seemed to have disappeared, leaving the crystalline sphere still atop the pedestal. The image of the city—the vast, gleaming city beneath the suns of Aetheria—still lingered in her mind, but it was the voice that interrupted her thoughts. *Find the Heart of Aetheria.* The voice was the same as the guide's from the forest. The figure from earlier had mentioned the Heart too. What was it?

She approached the pedestal and allowed her fingers to hover over the surface of the sphere. It felt cool to the touch, its soft glow calming her as she took a deep breath and tried to steady her thoughts.

Suddenly, the sphere flashed bright, momentarily

blinding her. Brea stumbled back, blinking rapidly as the cavern darkened. The light in the sphere flickered, dimming into a soft pulse like a heartbeat, and the temperature in the room dropped sharply.

From the shadows in the corners of the cavern, dark shapes began to emerge—vague, shifting forms that glided toward her. Brea's heart raced as the air around her thickened with their presence. She wasn't alone anymore.

"What—what is this?" she whispered, her voice shaky.

The shadows swirled, growing denser with every passing second, and a low, chilling whisper filled the air. It wasn't the same voice she'd heard before. This was darker, colder. The words were incomprehensible, but their intent was clear—this was no welcoming presence.

They're coming for you, her mind screamed.

Before Brea could react, the shadows lunged toward her. Instinctively, she held the book up with trembling hands. As soon as the book touched the open air, its familiar glow returned, brighter and more intense than before.

The shadows recoiled as the light spread across the cavern, pushing them back. Brea held the book tight to her chest, her heart pounding in sync with the sphere's soft pulsing glow.

The light from the book flared again, and in that moment, Brea felt something—an energy, a force, surging through her. It wasn't fear or panic, but something else, something... powerful. It was as if the book was unlocking a part of her she hadn't known existed.

The shadows hissed, retreating toward the edges of the cavern, their forms dissolving into the darkness. But Brea could feel them lingering just beyond the reach of the light, watching her, waiting.

"Why are they here?" she muttered under her breath, still clutching the book tightly.

A voice, clearer this time, echoed in her mind: *They are drawn to the Key, as all darkness is drawn to the light. But you are stronger than they are. You must trust in yourself, traveler.*

She stood there, breathing heavily, staring into the dark corners of the cavern where the shadows lurked. Trust in myself? She wasn't sure she could. None of this made sense —this world, the book, the shadows. She had never been someone who believed in magic or destiny, and yet… here she was.

The voice had said she was the Key, but what did that even mean? What power did she really have?

Taking another deep breath, Brea forced herself to calm down. Whatever was happening, she couldn't afford to fall apart now. She needed to find the Heart of Aetheria, and fast.

As if in response to her determination, the book in her hands began to hum with energy. Its glow intensified, and the pages fluttered open, revealing a new passage she hadn't seen before. The language was still foreign, but something inside her, something deep, seemed to under-stand it.

Brea's eyes skimmed the text, and the meaning of the words unfolded in her mind like a map: *To find the Heart, you must follow the Path of Shadows, where light and dark converge. Only there can the Key lock the gate.*

Her stomach twisted at the thought of following the shadows. But if the Heart of Aetheria was the key to understanding her role in this world, she didn't have a choice. She would have to face the darkness.

With the book still glowing in her hand, Brea made her way back toward the narrow path that had led her into the cavern. She didn't particularly like the idea of the long trek back through the mountain or crossing that bridge again, but she didn't have much of a choice.

Finally, as she stepped through the archway, the world outside had changed. The dim light that had once illuminated the landscape was gone, replaced by an inky blackness only lit by moonlight and the stars overhead. Long, eerie shadows were cast over the terrain.

Brea felt a chill creep down her spine as she looked around. The light that had once guided her was now so faint, and the shadows seemed thicker, more menacing. It was as if the world had shifted in response to the power she now knew she held.

Steeling herself, she took a step forward. The path before her wound back through the forest, the trees whispering in the wind as they swayed ominously. Every step she took was accompanied by the soft hum of the book, a reminder of the strange magic that now coursed through her.

The deeper she ventured into the forest, the darker the surroundings became. The shadows seemed to move of their own accord, curling and twisting around the trees, watching her. But she kept moving, gripping the book tightly in her hands.

As she walked, the path began to narrow, leading her into a thick fog that swirled around her feet. Her visibility shrank to almost nothing, and the whispers of the forest grew louder. It was as if the entire world was holding its breath, waiting for something to happen.

Suddenly, a voice—this time clear and distinct—broke through the oppressive silence.

"Traveler."

She froze, her heart racing. The voice was close, too close. She turned slowly, her eyes scanning the fog, but she saw nothing.

"Who's there?" she called, her voice trembling slightly.

There was no answer, only the sound of the wind rustling through the leaves.

Then, out of the fog, a figure appeared. It was shrouded in shadow, its features obscured. Brea took a cautious step back, her instincts screaming at her to run.

"You cannot escape your destiny," the figure said, its voice low and haunting. "You are the Key, but you are also the one who will bring the darkness."

Brea's blood ran cold. "What do you mean?"

The figure stepped closer, and for the first time, Brea could see its face—a reflection of her own, twisted in shadow.

"You will unlock the Heart of Aetheria," the figure whispered, its eyes glowing with a malevolent light. "But you will also unleash its greatest darkness. The choice is yours, traveler. Light or shadow. Life or death."

Brea's breath caught in her throat. *Light or shadow?* The words echoed in her mind, and in that moment, she realized the truth.

The path she was on wasn't just about saving Aetheria. It was about deciding its fate—and her own.

CHAPTER SEVEN

THE MIRROR OF FATE

Brea stared in disbelief at the shadowy figure before her. It wore her face, but twisted and distorted, as if darkness had claimed every part of her reflection. The glowing eyes bored into hers, pulsing with a cold light that sent a chill through her entire body.

She clenched the book tighter, feeling its warmth radiating against her palms, a comforting contrast to the icy presence of the figure. *Light or shadow? Life or death?* The figure's words echoed ominously in her mind, weighing heavy on her heart.

"What do you mean by that?" Brea asked, her voice trembling but steady enough to hold the fear at bay. "I don't understand."

The shadowy figure didn't immediately respond. Instead, it circled her slowly, its movements unnervingly fluid, as though it glided through the air rather than walked. As it moved, the fog thickened, closing in on Brea from all sides. The path she'd been following had completely disappeared, swallowed by the gloom.

"You hold the Key," the figure said finally, its voice low and hypnotic. "The power to unlock the Heart of Aetheria rests within you. But with that power comes a choice—light or shadow. Creation or destruction. Once the Heart is awakened, its true potential can only be realized through your decision."

Brea's heart pounded. "I don't want any of this. I didn't ask for power. I just... I just want to go home." Her voice cracked, betraying the growing panic she was trying so hard to suppress.

"There is no going back," the figure whispered, pausing directly in front of her. "This world, Aetheria, is now bound to you. Its fate is intertwined with yours. The Heart will soon be found, and when it is, you will stand at the crossroads."

The glowing eyes flickered as the figure tilted its head. "But not all who carry the Key choose wisely."

Before Brea could respond, the shadowy figure extended a hand toward her. Its fingers were long and thin, like wisps of smoke reaching out to her. The air around them seemed to hum with dark energy, and Brea felt a powerful pull, as if the shadows themselves were trying to claim her.

"You don't have to face this alone," the figure said softly. "There is strength in the darkness. It can give you power, more than you ever imagined. It can protect you from those who wish to use you. Together, we can rule this world. We can reshape it into something greater."

Brea recoiled, stepping back instinctively. The idea of wielding such power—of bending an entire world to her will—was both terrifying and strangely alluring. But something deep within her resisted. She wasn't a ruler. She wasn't meant to control others, to destroy or dominate.

"I don't want that," Brea said firmly, her voice steadier now. "I don't want power for its own sake."

The shadow figure's eyes flared, its expression twisting in a mixture of anger and amusement. "You think these people—this world—deserve to be saved? Look around you, traveler. This is a place of chaos, of constant conflict between light and shadow. You cannot have one without the other. And those who cling to the light will only betray you in the end. They always do."

Brea's thoughts drifted to the world she'd seen through the crystalline sphere—the grand city, the suns shining over the land. There had been beauty there, and a sense of hope. But there had also been shadows lurking beneath the surface, hidden in every corner, waiting for their moment to rise. Aetheria was more than just a land of light or darkness; it was both, entangled and inseparable.

"I don't believe that," she whispered, her eyes narrowing. "There's still hope, still goodness in this world. I've seen it. And if the Heart of Aetheria can bring balance, then that's what I'm going to do."

The figure sneered, the darkness around it writhing like a living entity. "You are naive. The Heart is not a tool of balance. It is a weapon—a weapon forged by the ancients to decide the fate of this world. Once it is awakened, it will either consume all in shadow or burn it in endless light. Either way, destruction will follow. There is no middle path."

Brea felt her chest tighten. Destruction. She hadn't considered that possibility. Could it be true? Could her choice—whether light or shadow—bring devastation no matter what she did?

But even as doubt began to creep in, the book in her hands pulsed again, its light flaring brighter than ever. The warmth of it seeped into her, spreading through her limbs and giving her the strength to stand firm.

"No," she said, her voice ringing clear. "I don't accept that. There is always a choice, and I will find a way to stop this. I won't let Aetheria be destroyed. I won't let it fall to darkness, or be consumed by light."

The shadow figure growled, its form shimmering with rage. "You fool! You don't understand what you're up against!"

Brea didn't back down. "Maybe not. But I'll figure it out."

Suddenly, the figure lunged at her, its smoky tendrils wrapping around her arms, pulling her toward the shadows. Brea struggled, but the more she resisted, the tighter the grip became. The book in her hands flickered, its glow dimming as the darkness threatened to smother her.

Just when it seemed the shadows would consume her

entirely, a blinding flash of light exploded from the book, cutting through the darkness like a blade. The shadow figure shrieked in agony, recoiling as the light burned through its form, dispersing it into the mist.

Brea collapsed to the ground, gasping for air as the last of the shadow melted away into the fog. The light from the book dimmed, but it remained steady, casting a protective glow around her.

As she struggled to her feet, a new thought struck her—what had just saved her? It wasn't just the book's magic; it was something deeper, something within her.

She glanced down at the book again, noticing for the first time that the pages had flipped to another passage. Her eyes scanned the text, and this time, she understood it perfectly: *The Heart is not found, it is earned. Only through facing the darkness within can the true path be revealed.*

Brea took a deep breath, her resolve hardening. The journey ahead wouldn't be easy, and the darkness wasn't just something out there in the world. It was inside her, too.

But she wasn't going to let it win.

With the Book in her hands and the words echoing in her mind, Brea set her sights on the next part of her journey. She would face the darkness, but she would do it on her own terms.

And somewhere, out there in the vast world of Aetheria, the Heart awaited her.

CHAPTER EIGHT

SHADOWS AND ALLIANCES

*B*rea had barely recovered from her encounter with the shadow figure when a sense of unease prickled at her skin. The fog that had briefly parted after the light's explosion began creeping back in, thicker and darker, twisting through the trees like ghostly fingers. The ancient woods that surrounded her felt more alive than ever, as if they were holding their breath, waiting for something—or someone.

She clutched the book tighter, its weight suddenly heavier in her hands. The passage she had read still echoed in her mind: *The Heart is not found, it is earned.* But what did it mean? How was she supposed to earn something that seemed more like a myth than reality?

The forest floor crunched beneath her boots as she cautiously moved forward, keeping her senses alert for any sign of danger. The soft light from the book had dimmed, but it still provided enough illumination to see the path ahead, winding through dense underbrush and ancient trees whose gnarled branches stretched toward the sky like skeletal arms.

Then, a sharp rustle cut through the silence, sending a jolt of adrenaline through Brea's veins. She froze, her heart racing. The sound was too deliberate, too precise to be caused by the wind.

Before she could react, another figure emerged from the shadows.

Tall, cloaked in midnight black, with silver hair that cascaded like moonlight over broad shoulders, the man who stepped forward was nothing short of mesmerizing. His dark, leather-clad form blended seamlessly with the shadows around him, and his eyes—icy blue and sharp—glinted with a mixture of curiosity and something far more dangerous. His presence seemed to command the very shadows, as if they bent and swirled in deference to him.

He stopped a few paces from Brea, one hand resting on the hilt of a wickedly curved sword that hung at his side. The sword's blade gleamed with a strange, dark energy that made Brea's skin crawl.

"Lost, are we?" His voice was low, smooth, and laced with dark amusement.

Brea's instinct screamed at her to run, but something about the man rooted her to the spot. His gaze, intense and unwavering, held hers captive. He exuded power—raw and magnetic—and though danger radiated from him like heat, there was something else beneath it, something she couldn't quite name.

"Who are you?" Brea asked, keeping her voice steady despite the unease coiling inside her.

The man's lips curled into a small, knowing smirk. "Who am I?" He tilted his head slightly, as if amused by the question. "Names have power in these lands, little wanderer. But since you ask…" He took a step closer, the shadows around him shifting and whispering in his wake. "You may call me Prince Ignatius."

"Prince?" Brea blinked, surprised. He didn't look like any prince she had ever imagined. There was no regal finery, no crown or jewel-laden cloak. He was dressed more like a warrior—hardened, dangerous, and utterly untrustworthy.

He must have sensed her hesitation because his smirk deepened, the corner of his lips pulling into a sharper, more dangerous smile. "Yes, prince," he repeated, his voice softening into something almost mocking. "Though my kingdom, like many things in this world, lies buried beneath layers of shadow."

Brea didn't know what to say. There was something hauntingly familiar about him, as if she had seen his face somewhere before, perhaps in one of the ancient tapestries she had glimpsed in the Whispering Wisp. He seemed to carry the weight of centuries in his eyes, a loneliness mingled with a dark, bitter wisdom.

"What do you want?" she asked, still wary. She tightened

her grip on the book, instinctively drawing it closer to her chest.

Ignatius' eyes flickered toward the book, a fleeting glance that didn't go unnoticed. "Ah, I see. So, you're the one with the Key." He didn't sound surprised, but there was a flicker of something else in his voice—interest, perhaps even intrigue. "I should have known the old crone wouldn't let just anyone find it."

Brea took a step back, her pulse quickening. "How do you know about the Key?"

Ignatius chuckled, a deep, velvety sound that sent shivers down her spine. "I know many things, little wanderer. The Heart of Aetheria, the Key, the ancient magic you now hold in your hands... they are all intertwined, threads in a much larger tapestry. A tapestry that I, too, have been seeking for quite some time."

He took another step closer, and Brea's breath hitched. His presence was overwhelming, as though he were more shadow than man. His gaze lingered on the book again, and Brea could feel the tension in the air grow thick between them.

"Don't be so quick to trust everything you've been told," Ignatius warned, his voice dropping to a whisper. "The Heart is not some sacred relic meant to bring balance to Aetheria. It is a weapon—a weapon that can either destroy this world or reshape it in ways unimaginable. And if you are truly the one destined to find it, then you will need more than just hope to survive the trials ahead."

Brea frowned, her mind spinning. A weapon? That's what the shadow figure had said as well. But why would Ignatius, this mysterious prince of shadows, care about what happened to the Heart? And more importantly—why did he care about her?

"Why are you telling me this?" she asked cautiously, her eyes narrowing.

Ignatius' smirk softened into something more dangerous —almost predatory. "Because, little wanderer, you and I are not so different. The world fears those who walk in the shadows, but it is we who understand its true nature. Light and shadow are not enemies; they are two sides of the same coin. And if you wish to survive, if you wish to control the power of the Heart, you will need someone who understands that balance."

Brea's heartbeat thundered in her ears. There was truth in his words, she knew that much. But there was also darkness, a darkness that tempted her. And yet, the thought of allying with someone like Ignatius—someone who seemed to straddle the line between savior and villain—was a risk she wasn't sure she could afford to take.

As if reading her thoughts, Ignatius stepped closer still, his voice a low, seductive whisper. "Join me. Together, we can reshape Aetheria. We can harness the Heart's power and ensure that neither light nor shadow dominates this land. But know this: the moment you refuse, others will come for you. And they will not be so kind."

Brea stared at him, her mind whirling with indecision.

The firelight from the book flickered faintly in her hand, casting shadows across the forest floor. She could feel the weight of the choice before her—join this enigmatic dark prince, or continue her journey alone.

Ignatius's gaze never wavered, his eyes gleaming with the promise of power, of shared destiny. "What will it be, little wanderer?" he asked, his voice a soft purr. "Light or shadow?"

Brea hesitated. The path ahead had never seemed so uncertain.

CHAPTER NINE

THE DARKNESS WITHIN

The choice hung in the air like a delicate thread—light or shadow. Brea felt the weight of Ignatius' gaze, his icy blue eyes burning with intensity. The dark prince, now standing close enough that she could feel the cold emanating from him, seemed to embody the shadows themselves. His offer was tempting, far too tempting, and Brea's mind was spinning with doubt. Ignatius. Even his name sounded ancient, wrapped in mystery. Brea shook her head, trying to focus. She didn't know this man, but what she did know was that he was dangerous.

"Why me?" Brea finally managed to ask, her voice quiet but firm. "What makes you think I can wield this power?"

Ignatius' lips curled into a smile that was both charming and sinister. "You underestimate yourself, little wanderer. The book chose you, did it not? The Key has long been lost to this world, hidden from those who seek it for selfish gain. But it appeared to you. That, in itself, makes you more than ordinary."

Brea frowned, gripping the book tightly as if it might slip from her hands. "But what do you want with it? You said the Heart is a weapon. What are you going to do with it?"

Ignatius took a slow step toward her, and the shadows seemed to follow his movement, swirling like mist at his feet. "What would you do if you had the power to reshape a world? If the balance of light and shadow were in your hands?"

Brea swallowed hard. She hadn't even thought that far ahead. All she wanted was to survive, to figure out why she'd been pulled into this strange world. But now, she was standing at the crossroads of destiny, with a man who exuded an air of authority and danger unlike anyone she had ever met.

"Answer me this," Ignatius continued, his voice a soft, dangerous whisper. "Do you believe this world deserves balance? Or would it be better to let it fall into chaos, where the strongest survive and the weak are devoured by their own ignorance?"

Brea didn't know how to respond. The world of Aetheria was as foreign to her as the language in the book, yet she could feel the pulse of something ancient and powerful within its pages. There was an undeniable connection between her and this place, but she was still grappling with the magnitude of it all. And Ignatius—he represented the unknown, the temptation to break free from the mundane and venture into a realm of limitless possibilities.

Before she could reply, the forest around them began to shift. The trees, once whispering softly, now creaked and groaned as if reacting to an unseen force. The mist thickened, coiling between the branches like serpents, and the air grew heavy with tension. Brea's grip on the book tightened instinctively.

Ignatius glanced around, his expression hardening. "We're not alone," he said, his voice losing its usual amusement. His hand moved to the hilt of his sword.

Brea's heart raced. She could feel it too, the presence of something dark and malevolent, lurking just beyond the veil of mist. The light from the book flickered, as if sensing the encroaching danger.

Without warning, a figure emerged, its form cloaked in darkness. It was tall and gaunt, with eyes like burning coals that glowed from beneath a hooded shroud. Its skeletal fingers extended toward Brea, and a low, guttural growl echoed through the trees.

Ignatius was quick to react, his sword flashing in the dim light as he stepped between Brea and the creature. The air hummed with power as the blade struck the creature's outstretched hand, sending a burst of dark energy rippling through the forest.

The creature recoiled with a hiss, retreating into the shadows, but not before its glowing eyes fixed on Brea. "The Heart... belongs to the Void," it rasped, its voice like the scraping of dry bones. Then, with a final snarl, it vanished into the mist, leaving only the echo of its words behind.

Brea's breath caught in her throat. The Void? She had never heard of such a thing, but the creature's words sent a chill through her. What exactly had she stumbled into?

Ignatius sheathed his sword, his eyes narrowing as he stared into the space where the creature had disappeared. "That was a Wraith of the Void," he said grimly, turning back to Brea. "They have been searching for the Heart for centuries. And now that you hold the Key to it, they will stop at nothing to take it from you."

Brea felt a cold sweat break out on her skin. "Why didn't you tell me this sooner?" she asked, her voice trembling with fear and frustration.

Ignatius's gaze softened, though the danger still lingered in his expression. "Would you have listened? The truth is, you are in the midst of a war, whether you wanted to be or not. There are those who would use the Heart to bring light and order, and those—like the Wraiths—who wish to plunge Aetheria into eternal darkness."

Brea took a shaky breath. "And where do you fall, Ignatius? Which side are you on?"

The question hung in the air for a moment, and Ignatius's expression darkened. He stepped closer, his presence overwhelming as he loomed over her. "I walk the line between light and shadow. I seek not the Heart for power, but for balance. Aetheria has suffered from the extremes of both.

And if you join me, Brea, we can restore that balance together."

Brea's mind was a whirlwind of thoughts and emotions. Ignatius was not like the Wraiths—of that much, she was certain. But his motives were shrouded in as much darkness as the shadows he commanded. Could she trust him? Or would aligning with him only pull her deeper into the abyss?

She looked up at him, searching his face for answers. His expression remained unreadable, though the intensity in his eyes never wavered. There was something almost vulnerable in that moment, as if he, too, was waiting for her to decide his fate as much as her own.

"What happens if I say no?" she asked softly.

Ignatius's lips twitched into a small, knowing smile. "Then you'll face the Void and the forces of light on your own. They will come for you. The Heart of Aetheria is too valuable, too dangerous to remain in the hands of an unaligned soul for long."

Brea's heart pounded in her chest. She didn't know what to believe anymore, but one thing was clear: she couldn't survive this alone. Not with the Wraiths hunting her, and certainly not with the weight of an entire world on her shoulders.

With a deep breath, she nodded. "Alright, Ignatius. I'll join you. But know this—I'm not your pawn. We're in this together, and if you try to betray me, I won't hesitate to stop you."

Ignatius's smile widened, though it didn't quite reach his

eyes. "A fair bargain," he said, extending his hand toward her. "Shall we begin?"

Brea hesitated only a moment before placing her hand in his, feeling the cool strength of his grip. The deal was made, and with it, her fate was sealed.

As the mist swirled around them, Ignatius's voice cut through the silence like a blade. "Welcome to the shadows, little wanderer. Our journey has only just begun."

CHAPTER TEN

THE WARDED CABIN

The sky above was now a patchwork of rolling storm clouds, their edges rimmed in silver as they loomed over the darkened landscape. The air was thick with the scent of rain, though the first drops had yet to fall. Brea tightened her grip on Ignatius, glancing over his shoulder as they rode, the tension between them as palpable as the storm on the horizon.

They had been riding for hours, leaving behind the mountain. While riding for such a period was draining and she was certain she'd never walk correctly again, she was even more grateful Ignatius had a horse. The ground had been unforgiving, the uneven terrain slowing their pace, but this was certainly better than walking all this way. The only sounds were the steady clop of hooves on dirt and the occasional rustle of leaves in the wind. Brea's mind churned with everything that had happened—the magic, the Heart, the relentless pursuit of the Void.

"We're almost there," Ignatius said, breaking the silence for the first time in what felt like hours.

Brea glanced up at him, her eyes lingering on the sharp lines of his face. His jaw was set, his eyes focused on the path ahead, as though he was determined to keep the distance between them—physically and emotionally. She wondered if he, too, felt the undercurrent of tension that had been simmering between them since the moment they had set out.

"Where exactly is 'there'?" she asked, her voice cutting through the stillness. "You've been vague about where we're going."

Ignatius's lips twitched into a faint smirk, though his eyes didn't leave the horizon. "There's a cabin. Deep in the woods, hidden from prying eyes. It's a place where we can regroup, rest, and plan our next move without worrying about the Void finding us."

Brea raised an eyebrow. "A cabin in the middle of nowhere?"

His smirk widened slightly, but it was laced with something darker. "Don't let the rustic charm fool you. The cabin's more than it seems. It's protected by old magic, wards that keep out those who don't belong."

That piqued her interest. "Wards?"

"Wards, yes," he said, his tone casual, but Brea knew there was more to the story than he was letting on.

As they rode deeper into the woods, the landscape

changed. The trees grew taller, their gnarled branches twisting overhead to form a dense canopy that blocked out the fading light of the day. Shadows danced between the trunks, and the air felt heavier, thick with the weight of old magic. The path narrowed, overgrown with vines and brambles, as if the forest itself was guarding the way to their destination.

Brea shivered, pulling the cloak Ignatius had given her tighter around her shoulders. "You sure we're going the right way?"

Ignatius gave her a sideways glance, the hint of amusement in his eyes. "You don't trust me?"

She narrowed her eyes at him. "Should I?"

Ignatius chuckled softly, the sound low and dark. "Fair enough. But yes, we're on the right path. The cabin is close."

They rode in silence again, but this time it wasn't the uncomfortable silence of earlier. There was something charged between them now, something that had been building since the moment they left the mountain. Brea could feel it in the way Ignatius glanced at her out of the corner of his eye, in the way his hand occasionally brushed against hers.

It was as if they were both aware of the storm brewing—not just in the sky, but between them.

The first drops of rain began to fall just as the cabin came into view, a small structure nestled deep in the heart of the woods. It looked ancient, its walls made of rough-hewn timber, the roof covered in moss and vines. But there was something about it, something that made Brea's skin prickle with the sensation of magic. She suspected she was feeling the wards Ignatius had mentioned, an invisible barrier that buzzed faintly in the air around the cabin.

They dismounted, the rain now coming down in a steady drizzle. Brea stiffly followed Ignatius to the door, her boots sinking slightly into the soft earth beneath her. He pushed open the heavy wooden door, and the scent of pine and old wood greeted them as they stepped inside.

The cabin was small but warm, a fire already crackling in the stone hearth as if it had been expecting them. Shelves lined the walls, filled with books and artifacts that looked far older than the cabin itself. A single table and two chairs sat in the center of the room, and a narrow staircase led up to what Brea assumed was a sleeping loft.

Ignatius hung his cloak on a hook by the door and turned to face her, his expression unreadable. "It's not much, but it'll do for the night."

Brea set the satchel Ignatius had given her down on the table, her fingers brushing over the rough wood as she glanced around. He claimed she couldn't go around just carrying the book around in the open.

The cabin felt lived-in, despite its remote location. "Whose place is this?"

"It belonged to someone I knew," Ignatius said, his voice lower than before. There was a hint of something in his tone—nostalgia, perhaps, or sadness—but he quickly masked it, moving to the hearth to tend to the fire.

"They're gone now, but the magic they left behind still holds."

Brea watched him in the firelight, the shadows playing across his sharp features. There was so much she didn't know about him, so many layers to the man who walked in the space between light and shadow. And yet, despite the danger he represented, there was a pull between them—a magnetic force that she couldn't quite explain, one that seemed to be growing stronger with each passing moment they were in each other's presence.

"Tell me something about you," Brea said.

Ignatius paused, his back to her. For a moment, she thought he might ignore the request. But then he turned, his eyes meeting hers, and the intensity in his gaze made her breath catch in her throat.

"My past is full of things better left forgotten," he said, his voice dark and laced with a kind of vulnerability that surprised her. "But not all of it. Some things… I hold onto."

Brea took a step closer, the tension between them palpable now, a current that hummed through the air. "Like this place?"

Ignatius nodded slowly, his eyes never leaving hers. "This place is a reminder. Of who I was… and who I could be."

Her heart raced, her pulse quickening as she took another step toward him. The space between them felt electric, charged with the weight of unspoken words and emotions that had been building since the moment they met. She didn't know why, but being close to him made her feel both terrified and exhilarated at the same time.

"Ignatius…" Brea whispered, her voice catching in her throat.

He stepped closer, closing the distance between them. His hand brushed against hers, the touch sending a shiver down her spine. His eyes darkened, his expression shifting into something more dangerous, more intimate.

"You should be careful with me," Ignatius said, his voice low and filled with a quiet intensity. "I'm not someone you should trust."

Brea's breath hitched. "I know. But I can't help it."

For a moment, it felt as though the world around them had stopped. The rain outside faded into the background, the crackling fire the only sound in the room. Brea's heart pounded in her chest as Ignatius's fingers lightly grazed her wrist, sending a surge of warmth through her body.

He leaned in, his breath warm against her skin. For a heartbeat, Brea thought he might kiss her, the tension between them snapping like a live wire. But instead, he pulled back, his eyes flicking toward the window as a sharp crack of thunder split the air.

"The storm's getting worse," he said, his voice returning to its usual calm, controlled tone. "We should rest. Tomorrow will be a long day."

Brea blinked, the moment shattered by the sudden shift. She nodded, her heart still racing, and moved toward the stairs that led to the loft. But as she climbed, she couldn't shake the feeling that something had changed between them —something that wouldn't be so easily forgotten.

The storm raged on outside, but inside the cabin, the air was thick with the promise of things left unsaid. And as Brea lay down on the simple bed in the loft, she couldn't help but wonder what it would mean for the journey ahead—both for her, and for Ignatius.

The shadows were closing in, and they were walking a dangerous line.

Together.

CHAPTER ELEVEN

DANCING ON THE EDGE

The crackling fire cast flickering shadows across the room as Brea sat across from Ignatius. The cabin was a temporary haven, a place where they could regroup, but the air inside felt heavier than it should have, thick with unspoken questions.

Ignatius, stoic as ever, had barely spoken since their heated moment the day before, and Brea had found herself wrapped in her thoughts. The weight of finding the Heart of Aetheria burned in her chest and it was as if the book itself was aware of the storm building between her and the dark prince.

Ignatius leaned back against the stone hearth, his sword resting by his side, though his posture remained taut, as though he was ready for whatever might come next. His sharp features were highlighted by the soft glow of the fire, and for the first time, Brea allowed herself to really look at him. He was undeniably handsome in a dark, dangerous way—his jaw sharp, his eyes cold and calculating, yet there was something else behind them, something that made her pulse quicken. Something wild.

She hadn't forgotten the way he'd protected her in the forest, the way he had stood between her and the Wraith, his power humming in the air like a live wire. But that same power made her wary. She couldn't forget who he was—a prince of shadows, walking the line between light and darkness. It made him unpredictable. Dangerous.

And yet, here they were, alone, the crackling fire the only witness to the tension that had been simmering between them since the moment they met.

"You're quiet." Ignatius finally said, his voice breaking the silence like a low growl. He didn't look at her, his eyes fixed on the fire, but she could feel the weight of his presence, drawing her in.

"I've got a lot on my mind," Brea replied, her voice steady, though her heart was racing. "Like how I've ended up in a magical world with a prince who walks in shadows, holding a book that every creature seems to want to kill me for."

Ignatius chuckled darkly, the sound sending a shiver down her spine. "Fair enough. But it's not just the book that draws them to you, little wanderer. You know that, don't you?"

She frowned, turning to look at him more closely. "What do you mean?"

He finally shifted his gaze to her, those icy blue eyes locking onto hers. The intensity of his stare sent a flush through her body, and she hated how easily he affected her. There was this edge to their interactions, a constant dance between attraction and danger.

"You're different," Ignatius said softly, his voice low, almost seductive. "The book chose you, and it wouldn't have done so without reason. There's something inside you—power you don't yet understand. It's not just the book that makes you valuable. It's you."

The way he said *you* made her stomach flutter, and Brea quickly looked away, trying to regain control over her spiraling thoughts. "You speak like you know me," she said, her tone sharper than she intended.

"I've been watching you since the moment you stepped into Aetheria." Ignatius's voice dropped to a near whisper. He leaned forward, resting his arms on his knees, his eyes never leaving hers. "I know more about you than you realize. You hide behind your fear, your doubts. But I see beyond that."

Brea's breath caught in her throat. There was something undeniably alluring about him—his confidence, the way he spoke as though he held all the answers. And yet, that same allure made her want to push him away. He was too close. Too dangerous.

"Ignatius, I'm not some... some puzzle for you to figure

out," Brea said, her voice shaking slightly. "I'm just trying to survive."

Ignatius smirked, but his eyes darkened with something deeper, something more primal. "Survival is one thing. Thriving is another. And I don't think you've ever allowed yourself to thrive, have you?"

Brea stood abruptly, unable to sit there under the weight of his stare any longer. The cabin felt stifling, the heat from the fire too much. She needed space. She needed air.

But as she moved toward the door, Ignatius was suddenly there, his presence overwhelming. He was close—too close—and the air between them seemed to crackle with an electric tension that made her heart race.

His hand came up, brushing a stray lock of her hair behind her ear, and the contact sent a jolt through her body. His touch was cool, but it ignited something deep inside her, something she couldn't quite control. "You're not alone in this. You don't have to be."

Her breath hitched, and she looked up at him, her eyes searching his for any hint of deception. But all she saw was that intensity, that hunger that mirrored her own confusion. She wanted to hate him. She wanted to push him away. But her body betrayed her, leaning into his touch, craving more.

"You're dangerous," she whispered, her voice barely audible over the crackling fire.

Ignatius's lips twitched into a small, knowing smile. "So are you."

Before she could think, before she could stop herself, Brea's hand found its way to his chest, feeling the hard muscle beneath his shirt. His breath hitched at the contact, and she saw a flicker of something—surprise, maybe, or desire—flash in his eyes.

Their faces were close now, their breaths mingling in the heated air between them. Brea could feel the tension building, a storm threatening to break, but she wasn't sure if she wanted it to. There was something intoxicating about being this close to him, about standing on the edge of something dark and unknown.

"Do you want this?" Ignatius asked, his voice a soft growl, his hand still resting on her cheek, his thumb tracing the line of her jaw. "Because once we cross this line, little wanderer, there's no going back."

Her heart raced, her mind screamed at her to run, to pull away. But her body, her heart, wanted more. And in that moment, the line between light and shadow blurred, leaving only the two of them, teetering on the edge of something they couldn't name.

"Ignatius…" she whispered, her voice trembling.

And then, before she could second-guess herself, she leaned in, closing the distance between them.

But just as their lips were about to meet, the door to the cabin burst open with a deafening crash, sending a gust of wind and rain swirling into the room. Brea jerked away, her heart pounding, and Ignatius's hand fell from her face as he spun around, sword already drawn.

A shadowed figure stood in the doorway, dripping wet from the storm outside, its eyes glowing red in the dim light.

"The Void sends its regards," the figure hissed, drawing a long, curved blade from its side.

The moment was shattered, and Brea felt the weight of reality slam back into her. The danger was still very real, and the world outside their fragile bubble of tension had come crashing back in.

CHAPTER TWELVE

BLADES OF THE VOID

The room was suddenly alive with tension, the crackling of the fire swallowed by the cold storm wind that howled through the open door. Brea's heart, which had just moments ago been racing for entirely different reasons, now thundered in her chest with pure adrenaline. The shadowy figure in the doorway advanced, its glowing red eyes locked on them, a dangerous, predatory gleam burning within them.

Ignatius stepped forward, his sword already raised, the deadly blade gleaming in the dim light of the cabin. "Get behind me," he ordered, his voice sharp and commanding, no trace of the warmth or tension from moments before. The dark prince had reverted to the warrior he truly was.

Brea, still shaken by the interruption, scrambled to her feet and took several steps back. Her fingers tightened around the book, feeling its pulse through her skin—a reassuring reminder that she wasn't defenseless. She could sense the darkness emanating from the intruder, a cold energy that mirrored the presence of the Wraith they had encountered earlier. This one, though, was different. Stronger.

The figure stepped fully into the cabin, the storm swirling behind it. Rain pounded against the wooden walls, but it was the icy voice that cut through the noise like a blade. "The Key is not yours to keep, Ignatius. Hand it over, and your life might be spared."

Ignatius chuckled darkly, his grip tightening on the hilt of his sword. "Do you think you can take it from me, Voidling? I've faced worse than your kind in my time." His voice dripped with disdain, but Brea could sense the seriousness beneath it. The danger was real, and they were outmatched if this creature was as strong as it seemed.

The Voidling snarled, raising its blade with a deadly swiftness. "Foolish prince," it hissed, stepping forward with menacing grace. "The Void will consume everything. You cannot resist forever. The Key and the Heart belong to the darkness, and they will return to us."

With a blur of motion, the Voidling attacked. Its blade moved like liquid shadow, swift and lethal, but Ignatius was faster. Their swords clashed with a sharp, metallic ring that echoed through the small cabin, sparks flying as they traded blows. The force of their battle sent tremors through the floor, and Brea watched in awe as Ignatius deflected strike after strike with fluid precision.

Despite the danger, there was something mesmerizing about the way Ignatius fought. His movements were graceful, almost like a dance, his dark cloak billowing around him as he sidestepped and countered the Voidling's relentless strikes. He was fierce, deadly, and completely in control, his every motion a testament to his skill and strength.

Brea's mind raced as she watched, knowing she couldn't just stand there, a helpless observer. She could feel the power of the book, the magic humming beneath its ancient pages, waiting for her to tap into it. But how? She wasn't Ignatius, with centuries of knowledge and experience. She didn't even fully understand the magic she held in her hands.

The clash of swords grew fiercer, the Voidling pressing its advantage with unnatural speed. Ignatius parried a strike aimed at his throat and retaliated with a powerful slash that sent the creature stumbling back. But Brea could see it—the exhaustion creeping into Ignatius's stance, the slight tremor in his arm as he fought to hold his ground.

He couldn't keep this up forever.

She took a deep breath, her pulse pounding in her ears. If she didn't act, they would both be killed. Ignatius, despite his power and strength, wouldn't be able to hold off this creature alone. And the Voidling wasn't just after him—it wanted the Key. It wanted *her*.

A surge of determination rushed through her. She had to act. She had to help him.

Brea focused on the book in her hands, feeling the magic coiling inside it, like a slumbering beast waiting to be awakened. She closed her eyes, letting her fingers trace the symbols on the pages, feeling the rhythm of the words as they pulsed beneath her skin.

Show me what to do, she thought, her mind reaching out to the magic within the book. *Help me.*

A strange warmth spread through her, the magic responding to her call. The pages of the book began to glow faintly, and she opened her eyes to see the text shifting, rearranging itself into something she could understand.

One word stood out, blazing with light: *Shield.*

Without thinking, Brea raised her free hand and whispered the word aloud. The magic surged through her, and in an instant, a shimmering barrier of light appeared between Ignatius and the Voidling, just as the creature's blade came down in a deadly arc.

The Voidling's sword slammed into the barrier with a crackling hiss, and the force of the impact sent it staggering back. It snarled in frustration, its glowing eyes burning brighter as it realized it had been thwarted.

Ignatius glanced back at Brea, his eyes wide with surprise —and something else. For a brief moment, she saw admiration flicker in his gaze, but it was gone as quickly as it came. He didn't waste time on words. With the Voidling off balance, Ignatius pressed the advantage, moving with lethal grace as he launched into another flurry of strikes.

Brea kept the shield in place, her heart racing with the effort of maintaining the spell. She could feel the strain of the magic pulling at her, but she didn't dare let it falter. The

Voidling was growing desperate, its attacks more frantic, but also more dangerous. It lunged at Ignatius again, its blade arcing toward his chest, but this time Ignatius was ready.

With a sharp, decisive movement, Ignatius parried the strike and brought his sword down with brutal force. The Voidling let out a screeching wail as the blade sliced through its shadowy form, and in a burst of dark energy, the creature disintegrated into nothingness, leaving only a swirling cloud of black mist behind.

For a moment, the cabin was silent except for the sound of their ragged breathing. The storm outside had quieted, the rain now a soft patter against the windows, and the fire crackled peacefully, as if the violent battle had never taken place.

Ignatius lowered his sword, his chest heaving as he turned to face Brea. His eyes were dark, but this time they were filled with something more than mere curiosity. There was a weight in his gaze, an intensity that made her breath catch.

"How did you do that?" he asked quietly, his voice rough from exertion.

Brea swallowed hard, the adrenaline still rushing through her veins. "I… I couldn't just stand by and watch. You needed help. I asked the book to help."

Ignatius took a step closer, his gaze never leaving hers. The air between them crackled with something more than just the remnants of magic. Brea's pulse quickened as he moved closer, his presence overwhelming her senses once again.

"You surprise me," he murmured, his voice low and husky.

Brea's breath hitched. There was something dangerous in his tone, something that made her heart race in a way that had nothing to do with fear. Ignatius was close now, close enough that she could feel the heat radiating from his body, could smell the faint scent of rain and steel clinging to him.

"You're not like anyone I've ever met, little wanderer," he said softly, his eyes boring into hers, full of that dark, magnetic intensity that drew her in despite herself. "And I find myself wanting to know more. To see what else you're capable of."

The weight of his words sent a thrill through her, but she fought to keep her composure. She couldn't afford to get lost in this—couldn't afford to let him get too close. But even as her mind screamed at her to put distance between them, her body betrayed her, leaning into his presence, craving the warmth and power that seemed to radiate from him.

"Ignatius…" she began, but her voice faltered.

His hand came up, once again brushing a strand of hair from her face, his touch featherlight but electric. "Careful, little wanderer," he whispered, his breath warm against her skin. "We're walking a dangerous line."

Her heart hammered in her chest as she stared up at him, torn between the storm of emotions swirling inside her. She wanted to push him away, but at the same time, she wanted to know what would happen if she didn't. If she let herself fall into the shadows with him.

But before she could make a decision, the sound of footsteps outside the cabin snapped them both back to reality.

Ignatius's expression hardened instantly, and he stepped back, sword at the ready again. Brea's pulse pounded in her ears as she gripped the book, the magic within it still humming, waiting.

Whoever—or whatever—was out there, they weren't alone anymore. And the danger was far from over.

CHAPTER THIRTEEN

THE GATHERING STORM

The door to the cabin creaked open again, and the wind howled as two figures stepped inside. They were cloaked in shadow, their forms blurred by the mist that had followed them in from the storm. Brea's heart raced, her fingers tightening around the book as she took a step back. Ignatius immediately moved in front of her, his sword raised, eyes sharp with anticipation.

One of the figures pushed back their hood, revealing a woman with striking features. Her skin was pale, almost ethereal, her hair jet-black and cascading down her back in loose waves. But it was her eyes that caught Brea's attention —ice blue, just like Ignatius's, but colder, if that was even possible. She stepped forward, ignoring the tension in the room, her gaze flicking between Ignatius and Brea.

"Ignatius," the woman said, her voice soft but commanding. "You're getting reckless. You know better than to leave loose ends."

Ignatius's posture stiffened, but he didn't lower his weapon. "What are you doing here, Lyra?"

Lyra. The name hung in the air, unfamiliar yet heavy with unspoken history. Brea could feel the tension between them, crackling like static. Whoever this woman was, it was clear she and Ignatius had a past—a complicated one.

"You didn't think I'd let you go off on this little adventure without me, did you?" Lyra's lips curled into a smirk, but her eyes remained cold, assessing. "This isn't something you can just keep to yourself. You know that."

Brea's stomach churned. What did this woman know? And more importantly, what did she mean about Ignatius keeping it to himself? Was there something Ignatius wasn't telling her?

Lyra's gaze shifted to Brea, and her smirk deepened. "And who's this?" she asked, her tone dripping with amusement. "I didn't realize you were taking on apprentices these days, Ignatius."

Brea bristled at the condescending tone, but before she could speak, Ignatius stepped in, his voice hard as steel. "She's not your concern, Lyra. Leave her out of this."

"Oh, but she is my concern," Lyra said, her eyes narrowing slightly. "You know the Key doesn't choose just anyone. If she's it, then she's more involved than you'd like to admit." Lyra's gaze locked onto Brea's, and the cold intensity in her eyes made Brea's skin prickle.

The second figure, who had remained silent up until now, finally stepped forward, pulling back his hood. He was tall, broad-shouldered, and his features were sharp, angular—handsome in a severe way. His hair was dark, and his eyes were a deep, unsettling green. There was a strange energy about him, one that made Brea instinctively take another step back. He exuded power, but not the same kind of darkness that Ignatius carried. This was something more calculated, more methodical.

"The Heart is dangerous," the man said, his voice calm and measured. "We can't let it fall into the wrong hands. And from what I've seen so far, that's exactly where it's headed."

Ignatius growled low in his throat, stepping forward to block their path further into the cabin. "You think you can take it? You're welcome to try."

The man smiled slightly, though it didn't reach his eyes. "I don't need to take it from you. The Key has a will of its own. It will choose its path in due time, and when it does, none of us will have control over it."

The cryptic words sent a chill down Brea's spine. She glanced down at the book in her hands, its familiar warmth still pulsing through her fingers. She had thought she was starting to understand it, starting to grasp the magic inside, but now she wasn't so sure. If what this man said was true, then the Key had a mind of its own, and the idea that it could choose anyone—any side—terrified her.

Ignatius tensed beside her, his sword gleaming in the

firelight. "You've always been arrogant, Caspian. But arrogance won't save you when the Void comes for you."

Caspian's smile faltered, but only for a moment. "And you think you're safe, Ignatius? You, who dances on the edge of both light and shadow? You're fooling yourself if you believe the Void will leave you untouched."

A sudden, sharp silence fell over the room. The storm outside had stilled, leaving only the crackle of the fire and the weight of unspoken truths hanging in the air. Brea's mind raced as she tried to piece together the fractured conversation.

"What is this about the Void?" Brea asked, her voice cutting through the tension. She hated feeling like an outsider in this conversation, like a pawn in a game she didn't understand. "What do they want with the Heart? Why am I so important?"

Lyra's eyes flicked back to Brea, her expression unreadable. "You truly don't know, do you?" she said softly, almost pitying. "The Heart of Aetheria is more than just a source of magic. It's a weapon. A weapon that can open realms beyond this one, places of power that have been locked away for centuries. Whoever controls the Heart controls the doors to those realms—and the power they hold. *You* are the Key to that weapon."

Brea's blood ran cold. She had known the Heart was powerful, but she hadn't realized the full extent of what it could unlock. Realms beyond this one? What kind of power was she holding inside her?

Caspian stepped closer, his green eyes piercing as they focused on Brea. "And the Void… they seek that power. They want to open the doors and unleash the darkness that's been sealed away. If they control the Heart, they will plunge Aetheria—and every other realm—into chaos."

Brea swallowed hard, her mind reeling. Everything felt like it was spiraling out of control. She had stumbled into this world without understanding the stakes, and now she was holding the key to something that could destroy entire worlds.

"Ignatius..." she whispered, her voice barely audible.

Ignatius's jaw tightened, his eyes still focused on Caspian and Lyra. "I didn't want to overwhelm you."

Lyra scoffed, crossing her arms. "You really are a fool, Ignatius. This is an ancient magic, older than any of us. She needs to be prepared and know what's at stake."

Brea felt a surge of panic rising in her chest. She had been so focused on surviving, on keeping herself safe, that she hadn't even considered the larger picture. The responsibility of what she was holding, the devastation it could bring—it was too much. She felt like she was drowning, sinking deeper into a sea of uncertainty and fear.

But Ignatius stepped closer, his hand reaching out to gently touch her arm. His touch was light, but the connection sent a ripple of warmth through her. His voice softened, no longer the cold, calculated tone he had used with the others. "We'll figure this out. You and I."

Brea looked up at him, her breath catching in her throat.

The intensity in his eyes was still there, but there was something else now—something that made her pulse quicken. For a moment, the rest of the world fell away. It was just the two of them, standing on the edge of something far more dangerous than any magic they had encountered.

She nodded slowly, the weight of his gaze grounding her. Whatever came next, they would face it together.

Caspian broke the silence, his voice sharp. "We don't have time for this. The Void is already moving. If we don't act soon, it won't matter what we do. Everything will fall to darkness."

Lyra moved to stand beside Caspian, her expression hardening. "You know he's right, Ignatius. The Void isn't waiting for us to figure out our little squabbles. If we don't stop them now, we'll all be swallowed by the shadows."

Ignatius's grip tightened on Brea's arm for a moment, then he turned to face the others. "Fine. We work together. But know this: if either of you tries to take the Heart for yourselves, I will kill you."

Lyra raised an eyebrow, unfazed. "Fair enough."

Caspian's eyes flicked to Brea, his gaze lingering on the book in her hands. "Then let's get moving. The storm is only just beginning."

CHAPTER FOURTEEN

THE UNRAVELING

The group left the cabin at dawn, moving through the mist-laden forest in tense silence. The storm had quieted, but the air remained thick with foreboding. Brea could feel the weight of the book in her satchel, pulsing softly like a second heartbeat, a constant reminder of the responsibility she now carried. Ignatius walked ahead of her, his movements deliberate, while Lyra and Caspian flanked them, their eyes scanning the surroundings for signs of danger. Brea couldn't help wishing they could've taken the horse. Brea was used to walking in the city, but hiking through the woods was entirely different. She was tiring much quicker than her companions, although her pride wouldn't let her show it.

Brea's mind raced with everything that had been revealed. The Heart wasn't just a magical artifact—it was the key to realms beyond Aetheria, realms filled with power that could reshape worlds. And the Void wanted that power, wanted to plunge everything into chaos. It was too much to process all at once, and every step forward felt like she was falling deeper into a trap she hadn't seen coming.

"Ignatius," Brea whispered, quickening her pace to walk beside him, "what happens if the Void gets the Heart? What does that mean for Aetheria?"

He glanced at her, his jaw set in a hard line. "If the Void gets the Heart, it means the end. They'll open the gates to the other realms and flood Aetheria with darkness. Every creature of shadow, every dark force that has ever been sealed away, will pour into this world." He paused. "That is, if they have you as well to unlock the Heart."

Brea's stomach churned. "So we're not just fighting for Aetheria, are we? We're fighting for every world connected to this one."

Ignatius gave a grim nod. "Exactly."

As they walked, Brea couldn't shake the feeling that they were being watched. The forest always felt alive, the mist curling through the trees like grasping fingers, but it was more than that. She sensed something moving in the shadows, just beyond her sight. Every rustle of leaves, every faint creak of branches set her nerves on edge.

"How far is this place?" Lyra asked from behind them, her tone sharp. "We need to move faster. The Void isn't going to wait for us to catch our breath."

Ignatius's eyes flicked back at her, but his tone remained calm. "We're close. Patience."

Lyra rolled her eyes but said nothing further. Caspian, on the other hand, had been eerily quiet since they left the cabin. His presence unnerved Brea in a different way than Ignatius's did. Where Ignatius's darkness was dangerous but magnetic, Caspian's was more calculating, as if he was always two steps ahead, planning his next move. Brea couldn't help but wonder what he was hiding beneath that calm exterior.

They pressed on, the silence between them growing thicker, but the tension shifted when they reached a clearing. The mist parted to reveal a vast chasm ahead, its depths lost in swirling shadows. The ground fell away into nothingness, and across the chasm, a towering structure loomed—an ancient fortress, its stone walls dark and imposing. Tendrils of mist clung to the fortress like ghostly fingers, and the air around it seemed unnaturally still.

Brea felt a chill crawl down her spine. "What is this place?"

Ignatius stopped at the edge of the chasm, his eyes fixed on the fortress. "The Void Gate," he said quietly. "It's one of the places where the barriers between realms are weakest. If they continue to get through that gate, there will be nothing to stop them."

Lyra crossed her arms, her expression unreadable. "And how exactly are we supposed to stop them?"

Caspian finally spoke, his voice low and calm. "The Void Gate can't be destroyed, but it can be sealed. Temporarily.

We just need to make sure it stays closed long enough to secure the Heart and prevent them from using it."

Brea's heart pounded as she looked at the gate. It felt like they were standing on the edge of the abyss—both literally and figuratively. "And what do I do?" she asked, her voice small.

Ignatius glanced at her, his eyes softening for just a moment. "You stay close. But I don't want you getting too close to the Void's magic. It's… unpredictable."

Lyra snorted. "Unpredictable? That's putting it lightly."

Ignoring her, Ignatius turned back to Brea. "Just trust me. We'll face this together."

Brea's breath hitched. There it was again, that pull between them, the magnetic force that seemed to bind them in a way she couldn't explain. Every time he looked at her like that, it felt like the rest of the world faded away, leaving only the two of them standing on the brink of something both dangerous and thrilling.

But before she could respond, a low, rumbling sound echoed from the chasm. The ground beneath their feet trembled, and the shadows within the chasm began to shift, swirling faster, darker. The Void was stirring.

"They're coming," Caspian said, his voice cold and matter-of-fact. He stepped forward, his hands glowing faintly with magic as he prepared for the fight ahead.

Lyra unsheathed a pair of twin daggers, her expression hard. "Looks like we don't have much time."

Ignatius's grip tightened on his sword, his jaw clenched in

anticipation. "We hold them here. Keep them away from the gate as long as possible."

Brea's heart raced as she watched the shadows twist and writhe, growing darker by the second. The air itself seemed to thicken with the weight of the Void's presence, and every instinct in her body screamed at her to run. But she couldn't. She had to stand her ground. She had to face whatever was coming.

The first of the Void's creatures emerged from the chasm, a monstrous figure wreathed in darkness. Its glowing red eyes burned through the mist as it climbed over the edge, followed by more shadowy forms. Brea's breath caught in her throat as she watched the creatures pour out, one after another, until the clearing was filled with them—twisted, nightmarish beings made of shadow and malice.

Caspian moved first, unleashing a torrent of magic that slammed into the creatures, sending several of them sprawling back into the abyss. Lyra followed suit, her daggers flashing in the dim light as she cut down anything that got too close.

Ignatius was a blur of motion, his sword slicing through the air with deadly precision. He fought like a force of nature, his movements graceful yet brutal, cutting down every creature that dared approach him. Brea couldn't tear her eyes away from him, even as fear gripped her heart. He was terrifyingly beautiful in battle—deadly and mesmerizing.

But the creatures kept coming, wave after wave of them,

and no matter how many they cut down, more seemed to take their place. Brea felt the pull of the Book growing stronger, the magic within it awakening in response to the Void's presence.

Suddenly, one of the creatures broke through their line, lunging directly at Brea. She stumbled back, her heart pounding in her chest as the monster bore down on her, its red eyes glowing with malice.

"Brea!" Ignatius shouted, but he was too far away, locked in battle with another creature.

Without thinking, Brea raised the book in her hands, whispering the words she had barely understood before. The magic surged through her, and a burst of light exploded from the Book, slamming into the creature and sending it flying back into the chasm.

Brea gasped, her chest heaving from the effort. The power was overwhelming, filling her veins with fire, but she could feel it slipping, could feel the darkness creeping in around the edges of her mind.

"Ignatius!" she called out, her voice desperate. "I don't know how much longer I can hold this."

Ignatius cut down the last of the creatures in his path and rushed to her side, his expression fierce and protective. "Stay with me, little wanderer," he said, his voice urgent but steady. "We're almost there. Just a little longer."

But before he could say anything else, the ground shook violently, and a deep, guttural roar echoed from the chasm.

Brea's eyes widened as she looked down, her heart stopping at the sight of what was rising from the darkness.

A massive, hulking figure wreathed in shadows, its eyes burning with the pure, unrelenting fury of the Void. It was unlike anything they had faced so far—bigger, stronger, and filled with a malevolent power that made the air crackle with energy.

"That," Caspian said, his voice grim, "is what we've been trying to keep at bay."

The creature stepped onto the edge of the chasm, towering over them, and let out another earth-shattering roar. Brea could feel the book pulsing wildly in her hands, its magic struggling to contain the power of the Void that threatened to consume everything.

And in that moment, she realized just how high the stakes truly were.

CHAPTER FIFTEEN

INTO THE ABYSS

The ground trembled beneath Brea's feet as the monstrous figure towered over them, its hulking form cloaked in shadows so thick they seemed to swallow the light. The roar it unleashed was more than just a sound— it was a force that vibrated through the air, shaking the very core of her being. The magic from the book pulsed violently in her hands, its energy swirling in response to the overwhelming presence of the Void.

"Ignatius!" Brea shouted over the deafening roar. Panic gripped her chest like a vice, but she forced herself to focus, to cling to the small flicker of control she had over the book's magic.

Ignatius, standing protectively beside her, gripped his sword tightly, his eyes locked on the massive creature emerging from the depths of the chasm. His jaw was set in a grim line, and for the first time, Brea saw something in his expression that unnerved her: doubt.

Lyra and Caspian were already on the move, both of them attacking with swift, practiced precision. Lyra's twin daggers flashed as she darted toward the creature, moving with the grace of a shadow. Caspian unleashed powerful bursts of magic, his hands glowing with an eerie light as he hurled spell after spell at the Void's monstrosity. But the creature barely flinched, shrugging off their attacks as if they were nothing more than annoyances.

"This isn't working!" Lyra shouted, dodging a massive swing of the creature's arm that sent the ground cracking beneath her feet.

"We have to close the gate!" Caspian called out, his voice strained as he unleashed another torrent of magic. "As long as it's open, they'll keep coming!"

Brea's heart raced. Close the gate? But how? The Void Gate loomed on the other side of the chasm, a towering structure of stone and shadow, its ancient power radiating across the battlefield. She could feel its pull, its dark energy reaching out to her, tempting her, whispering promises of power.

The massive creature roared again, and in that moment, its glowing red eyes locked onto Brea. It sensed the Key, its gaze filled with a hunger that sent a wave of cold terror down her spine.

"It's coming!" Brea gasped, backing away instinctively as

the creature lumbered toward her, its movements slow but unstoppable.

Ignatius stepped in front of her, his sword raised. "We're not letting it take you." His voice was low, determined, but there was something darker in his tone—something more personal, as if he would rather die than let the Void claim her.

The creature swung its massive arm toward them, and Brea barely had time to react. Ignatius deflected the blow with a powerful swing of his sword, the clash of metal against shadow ringing through the air. The force of the impact sent Ignatius staggering back, but he held his ground, his eyes blazing with fierce resolve.

"You need to close the gate!" Ignatius shouted over his shoulder, his voice edged with urgency. "The book—use it! It's the only way!"

Brea's breath caught in her throat. She had no idea how to do that. She barely understood how to control the book's magic, let alone use it to close a gate to another realm. But there was no time to hesitate. If they didn't stop the Void now, it would consume everything.

Her mind raced, and she felt the weight of the book in her hands, its warmth growing more intense as the Heart reacted to the danger around them. The magic hummed, alive and ready, waiting for her to command it. But how? How did she unlock the power that could close the gate?

Another roar from the creature jolted her back to the

present. It was closing in, its glowing red eyes fixed on her, each step shaking the ground beneath it.

"You can do this!" Ignatius's voice cut through her panic. "Trust yourself!"

She met his gaze for a brief moment, and something inside her clicked. Trust. The same way the book had responded to her before, when she needed to protect them. The same way it had saved them from the Void's creatures. This power wasn't just something inside the book—it was connected to her, a part of her.

Taking a deep breath, Brea closed her eyes and focused. She felt the pulse of the book in her hands, its magic flowing through her, and she let herself sink into that connection. Slowly, she reached out with her mind, searching for the power that lay within the book's ancient pages.

As she did, the words she had seen before began to form in her mind—ancient, powerful words that seemed to resonate with the very essence of the world around her. She didn't know what they meant, but they filled her with a sense of purpose, of clarity.

Opening her eyes, Brea lifted the book, her voice steady as she spoke the words aloud.

"Avorah Shal Varin! Sokathor Un Ereth!"

The moment the words left her lips, the air around her changed. The magic surged through her, and the world seemed to shift. The shadows recoiled as a wave of light exploded from the book, rippling across the clearing with a force so strong that it sent the Void creatures tumbling back into the abyss.

The massive creature in front of her roared in fury, but it couldn't get any closer. The magic pushed it back, creating a barrier of light that separated it from Brea and her companions.

The Void Gate trembled, its stone walls cracking as the power of the Book surged through the air. The gate began to close, slowly, the shadows retreating as the barrier between realms grew stronger.

"You're doing it!" Ignatius shouted, his voice filled with awe and urgency.

But it wasn't over yet. The massive creature, sensing its defeat, let out one final, deafening roar. It raised its massive arms, and with a last, desperate lunge, it threw itself toward Brea, its claws outstretched, aiming for the Book.

Brea gasped, the force of the creature's attack shaking her concentration. The magic wavered, and the barrier of light flickered.

"NO!" Ignatius roared, his sword flashing as he leapt between her and the creature.

The impact was brutal. The creature's claws slammed into Ignatius's chest, sending him crashing to the ground with a sickening thud. Brea's heart stopped as she watched him fall, his sword slipping from his grasp, blood staining the ground beneath him.

"IGNATIUS!" Brea screamed, her voice filled with raw terror.

She felt the magic surge again, stronger this time, fueled by her fear and anger. The magic responded to her emotions, and the words she had spoken before burned brighter in her mind. With a cry, she unleashed even more power.

A blinding light erupted from the book, engulfing the entire clearing. The creature was caught in the blast, its form disintegrating into nothingness as the magic tore through it. The Void Gate sealed with a thunderous crack, the chasm closing as the darkness was forced back into the abyss.

And then, silence.

Brea stood frozen, the book still glowing faintly in her hands, her heart pounding in her chest. The air was still, the battle over, but her mind was consumed with one thought.

Ignatius.

She dropped to her knees beside him, her hands trembling as she reached for him. His chest was slick with blood, his breathing shallow, and for the first time, the confident, unshakable man she had come to rely on looked fragile. Vulnerable.

"Ignatius," she whispered, her voice breaking as tears filled her eyes.

His eyes fluttered open, and he gave her a weak smile, his hand reaching up to touch her cheek. "You did it," he rasped, his voice barely audible.

Brea shook her head, tears spilling down her cheeks. "Stay with me. Please."

Ignatius's fingers brushed her skin, and for a moment, the

intensity in his gaze was as fierce as ever. But then, his eyes closed, his hand falling limp in hers.

"No," Brea whispered, her voice cracking. "No, no, no…"

The light from the book flickered, dimming as the weight of the moment pressed down on her. The battle was won, but at what cost?

Tears streamed down her face as she knelt beside him, her heart breaking.

CHAPTER SIXTEEN
HEART OF DARKNESS

Brea knelt beside Ignatius, her heart heavy with grief as she held his limp hand in hers. The world around her seemed to blur, the remnants of battle fading into an indistinct haze. The only thing she could focus on was the shallow rise and fall of his chest, his breathing weak but still there—still fighting. Her tears splashed onto his bloodstained skin, her throat tight with a mix of anger, fear, and a desperate hope that he would survive.

"Ignatius, please…" she whispered, her voice trembling. She clutched the book in her other hand, its warmth dimming as her own strength faltered. "You can't leave me. Not now. Not like this."

Beside her, Lyra and Caspian watched in silence, their expressions unreadable. The battle was over, the Void Gate sealed, but the cost had been high. The threat of the Void still lingered, a shadow that stretched across Aetheria, and Ignatius—strong, confident Ignatius—was slipping away before her eyes.

Lyra stepped forward, her face hard but her eyes softer than usual. "We don't have time for this," she said, her voice low. "If we're going to survive, we need to move. Now."

Brea wiped her tears, a sudden anger flaring inside her. "I'm not leaving him behind!"

Caspian glanced at Lyra, his expression tight. "We're not suggesting that. But the magic of the Void won't stay contained forever. We have to get to safety before the Gate begins to unravel. If we don't leave now, none of us are getting out of here alive."

Brea bit her lip, torn between the urgency of their situation and her desperation to keep Ignatius alive. She looked down at him, his face pale, his breaths shallow. The darkness of the Void still clung to him like a shadow, its tendrils slowly draining the life from him.

Without thinking, Brea gripped the book tighter, feeling its faint pulse in her hand. She didn't know if it could save him, but it was her only hope.

"What are you doing?" Lyra asked, her eyes narrowing as she watched Brea lift the book over Ignatius's chest.

"I'm going to try something," Brea said, her voice quiet but determined. "The book—it's connected to me. Maybe it can heal him, maybe it can... I don't know, reverse the damage the Void has done."

Caspian stepped forward, his eyes wide with concern.

"That kind of magic is dangerous. It doesn't just give; it also takes. If you try to channel its power, you could—"

"I don't care!" Brea snapped, her voice breaking. "I'm not losing him. I won't!"

Lyra crossed her arms, watching with narrowed eyes but not interfering. "Then do it. But you better be ready to accept whatever price the magic demands."

Brea barely heard her. She closed her eyes, focusing on the warmth of the Book in her hands, letting its magic flow through her. The power stirred deep within the book, awakening in response to her need. She could feel it thrumming beneath the surface, a well of ancient energy that called to her, beckoning her to reach into its depths.

With a deep breath, Brea opened her eyes and whispered the words that came to her mind, unbidden but familiar, as if they had always been there, waiting for her to find them.

"Vathiel En Sareth, Revian Tul Marith!"

The book glowed fiercely, its light illuminating the clearing as tendrils of magic flowed from the book and wrapped around Ignatius's still form. The air around them crackled with energy, and Brea felt the power of the book surge through her veins, connecting her to Ignatius, to the magic of Aetheria itself.

For a moment, everything stilled. The world seemed to hold its breath as the magic worked its way through him, knitting together the wounds left by the Void, fighting against the darkness that sought to claim him.

But then, as quickly as it had come, the light dimmed.

The magic receded, leaving Brea breathless and drained. She slumped forward, her hands trembling as the book slipped from her grasp.

"Did it work?" Lyra asked, her voice breaking the heavy silence.

Brea didn't answer, her gaze locked on Ignatius's face. His breathing had slowed to a faint rhythm, but he wasn't awake. His chest still rose and fell, but the darkness hadn't fully left him. The Void's poison clung to him, refusing to release its hold.

"I don't know," Brea whispered, her voice thick with exhaustion. "It's not enough. I can't—"

"He's alive," Caspian said, stepping closer to inspect him. "But he's not out of danger. We need to get him somewhere safe, where the Void can't reach him."

Brea nodded weakly, her limbs heavy from the strain of using the Book's magic. She had tried—she had given everything—but it hadn't been enough. Ignatius was still on the edge of life and death, and time was slipping away.

Lyra knelt beside her, her sharp gaze softening slightly. "You did what you could. Now let's get him out of here."

Brea wanted to argue, wanted to fight, but the truth was undeniable. She had done everything in her power, and it still wasn't enough to pull Ignatius from the darkness that had claimed him.

With trembling hands, Brea lifted the book once more, tucking it carefully back into her satchel. Caspian and Lyra moved to lift Ignatius between them, carrying him toward the edge of the clearing. Brea followed close behind, her heart heavy with guilt and fear.

As they reached the edge of the forest, Caspian spoke in a low voice. "There's a place we can take him. A sanctuary. It's hidden deep within the mountains, far from the reach of the Void. The magic there is ancient, powerful. If anything can heal him, it's that place."

"Then let's go," Brea said, her voice barely above a whisper.

The journey was long and grueling. The night seemed to stretch endlessly as they made their way through dense forests and treacherous terrain. Brea stayed close to Ignatius, her hand brushing his from time to time, checking his pulse, listening for his breath. He remained unconscious, teetering between life and death, his skin pale and cold to the touch.

The sanctuary Caspian had spoken of finally came into view just as the sun began to rise, casting a faint golden light over the mountains. It was a place of beauty and stillness, hidden among towering peaks and waterfalls. The air was crisp and pure, and Brea could feel the ancient magic humming through the earth beneath her feet.

Lyra and Caspian carried Ignatius into the heart of the sanctuary, where an ancient altar stood, surrounded by towering stone pillars. The magic here was palpable, a force that seemed to pulse with life itself.

"This is it," Caspian said, his voice reverent. "If there's any place that can save him, it's here."

Brea knelt beside the altar, her hand resting on Ignatius's

chest. "Please," she whispered, her voice cracking. "Please, come back."

The magic of the sanctuary stirred, wrapping around Ignatius like a protective shield. The air shimmered with power, and Brea felt the faint pulse of the book, as if it too was connected to this place.

For what felt like an eternity, they waited in silence, watching the magic work, hoping, praying.

And then, slowly, painfully, Ignatius's eyes fluttered open.

His gaze was unfocused at first, but then it locked onto Brea, and a weak smile tugged at the corners of his lips.

"You never give up, do you?" he rasped, his voice barely audible but filled with the familiar dark amusement she had come to know.

Brea let out a sob of relief, her heart bursting with emotion. "You're alive," she whispered, tears spilling down her cheeks. "You're alive."

Ignatius's hand found hers, squeezing it weakly.

Brea's heart soared, but the weight of their journey—and the battles yet to come—still lingered. Ignatius was alive, but the Void was still out there, and the Heart of Aetheria was still a weapon that could bring unimaginable destruction.

As she knelt beside him, their hands intertwined, Brea knew their fight was far from over. The darkness had only just begun to stir, and they would need each other more than ever to face what was coming.

CHAPTER SEVENTEEN
SHADOWS UNVEILED

The sanctuary's air hummed with ancient magic, and although Ignatius was breathing steadily now, the weight of what lay ahead settled heavily on Brea's shoulders. She sat beside him, their hands still intertwined, feeling the warmth of his touch as if it was tethering her to reality after the chaos of battle.

Ignatius stirred, slowly propping himself up on his elbows, his body weak but recovering. His gaze was softer now, the fierce intensity momentarily replaced by vulnerability. For a moment, the prince of shadows seemed almost human, stripped of the darkness that always clung to him like a second skin.

"You saved me again," Ignatius said, his voice hoarse but filled with something close to admiration.

Brea nodded, her heart still heavy with the knowledge

that she had come so close to losing him. "I didn't have a choice. I couldn't let you die."

His fingers brushed against hers, a gentle touch that sent a ripple of warmth through her. Ignatius's eyes, though weary, held a flicker of that familiar spark—the one that made her feel like she was teetering on the edge of something dangerous. And thrilling.

"You keep surprising me," he said, his lips curving into a small, tired smile. "You have more power than you realize."

Brea looked away, her thoughts swirling. The magic had responded to her, yes, but the feeling of that magic coursing through her had been overwhelming, almost too much to bear. She had felt as though she was standing on the precipice of something vast and uncontrollable, and it had scared her.

"I don't know what I'm doing," she admitted quietly, pulling her hand back from his. "I don't understand any of this—this power, this magic. What if I lose control? What if... what if I destroy everything instead of saving it?"

Ignatius's gaze softened, but he didn't try to comfort her with empty reassurances. Instead, he shifted to sit up fully, wincing slightly from the pain of his injuries but determined nonetheless. "The Heart is dangerous. You know that now. But you're stronger than you think."

His words hung in the air between them, heavy with meaning. Brea met his eyes again, and for the briefest moment, she allowed herself to believe that maybe—just maybe—she wasn't as lost as she felt. Maybe, with Ignatius by her side, she could find her way through this darkness.

A cough from the other side of the room broke the moment, and Brea turned to see Lyra standing with her arms crossed, her expression as sharp as ever. Caspian stood beside her, his green eyes unreadable as he watched the exchange.

"Well, if you two are done with your heartfelt reunion," Lyra said, her tone clipped, "we have bigger problems to deal with."

Brea bristled at the interruption, but Ignatius chuckled softly, the sound rough but full of amusement. "Always so charming, Lyra."

Lyra rolled her eyes. "We don't have time for charm, Ignatius. The Void won't stop just because you got a second chance. We sealed the Gate, but you know as well as I do that it's only a temporary fix. The Void is still out there, and they'll come for her again. Sooner or later."

Brea's stomach tightened. She had known this wasn't over, but hearing it said out loud made it all the more real. The Gate may have been closed, but the threat was far from contained. The Void was still lurking, waiting for another opportunity to strike.

"And there's something else," Caspian added, his voice low and measured. "While you were... recovering, we received word from our informants. There's movement in the east. The Void's forces are gathering, preparing for something."

Ignatius's eyes sharpened, the soft vulnerability from moments ago replaced by the warrior's edge she had come to know. "What kind of movement?"

Caspian exchanged a glance with Lyra before speaking again. "A convergence. Dark magic is pooling in the region near the ancient ruins of Valcora. It's as if the Void is trying to tap into an even older power—something from before the realms were separated."

Brea felt a chill run down her spine. "Older than the realms? What does that mean?"

Lyra's expression turned grim. "It means the Void isn't just after the Heart. They're after the source of all magic in Aetheria. If they succeed, they won't need to open the Gate again. They'll have the power to tear the realms apart."

Ignatius's jaw clenched, his mind clearly racing. He pushed himself to his feet, though Brea could see the strain it caused him. "We need to move. If the Void is planning something at Valcora, we can't afford to sit here and wait. We have to stop them."

Caspian raised an eyebrow. "You're in no shape to lead a battle, Ignatius. You can barely stand."

Ignatius shot him a dark look, his pride flaring. "I'll be fine."

Brea stood up as well, stepping closer to him. "You're not fine, Ignatius. You're still recovering. You need time—"

"I don't have time," he interrupted, his voice low and filled with frustration. "None of us do. The Void isn't waiting for me to heal."

His words were harsh, but Brea understood. The weight of the world was pressing down on him just as it was on her. They were all fighting against forces that seemed impossible to defeat, and every moment of hesitation felt like a step closer to disaster.

Lyra sighed, uncrossing her arms. "You're stubborn as ever, but Caspian's right. You're not at full strength. We need a plan."

"I'll go," Brea said, surprising herself with the conviction in her voice.

Ignatius and the others turned to her, their expressions a mixture of surprise and concern.

"I don't think—" Ignatius began, but she cut him off.

"I'm the Key," she said, her hand resting on the satchel where the book lay. "The Heart is connected to me, and if the Void is gathering power, then I have to be there. This is my fight too."

Lyra raised an eyebrow, her lips twitching into a faint smirk. "Look at that, the little wanderer is growing a backbone."

Brea shot her a glare, but Ignatius was the one she was focused on. His eyes searched hers, conflicted.

"You don't have to do this," he said softly, stepping closer to her. "Not alone."

"I won't be alone," Brea replied, her voice steady. "We're in this together. All of us. But we can't let the Void win."

Ignatius was silent for a long moment, his gaze intense.

Then, slowly, he nodded, the fight still burning in his eyes. "Alright. We do this together."

Caspian cleared his throat, drawing their attention. "If we're going to Valcora, we need to leave now. The Void's forces are already gathering, and we can't afford to fall behind."

Lyra nodded in agreement. "We'll head east at first light."

The decision was made, and the tension in the air shifted once more. The battle wasn't over—it had only just begun. But this time, Brea wasn't just following Ignatius. She was standing beside him, ready to face whatever darkness lay ahead.

As they prepared to leave, Brea felt a flicker of resolve ignite within her. The Heart of Aetheria was more than just a weapon, more than a key. She would wield its power—not for herself, but to protect Aetheria from the shadows that sought to consume it.

Ignatius caught her gaze again, his eyes dark and unreadable, but there was something in the way he looked at her now, something more than just duty. There was a connection, a shared understanding that went beyond words.

"Stay close," he said, his voice low and intimate. "I won't let anything happen to you."

Brea nodded, her heart racing at the intensity in his gaze. "You'll have to keep up with me."

Ignatius's lips curved into a small, dangerous smile. "Challenge accepted."

CHAPTER EIGHTEEN

THE ROAD TO VALCORA

The road to Valcora stretched out before them, a winding path through rugged terrain and shadowed woods, the air thick with the scent of rain and earth. Brea walked at the center of the group, her eyes fixed on the horizon where distant storm clouds gathered. The atmosphere was heavy, not just from the coming weather but from the knowledge that they were walking toward something far more dangerous—an impending confrontation with the Void.

Ignatius walked beside her, silent and brooding as always, his dark cloak billowing slightly in the wind. The intensity in his gaze had only deepened since they had left the safety of the cabin, his focus entirely on the mission ahead. The others —Lyra and Caspian—walked behind, their expressions equally grim. They all knew what was at stake.

Valcora was once a city of great power, a place where the ancient magic of Aetheria had thrived. But now it lay in ruins, its bones scattered across a vast plain, and its magic, though long dormant, was still potent enough to draw the attention of the Void. The idea that the Void was gathering there, seeking to tap into the ancient power for their own ends, sent chills down Brea's spine.

"What's our plan when we get there?" Brea asked, breaking the silence that had settled over the group like a shroud.

Ignatius glanced at her, his jaw tightening. "We assess the situation first. We don't know how many forces the Void has gathered, or how far they've gone in unlocking Valcora's magic. We'll need to act quickly—before they gain control of it."

Lyra, walking slightly behind them, snorted. "You mean we don't know how badly we're outnumbered. Let's be honest, Ignatius. We're walking into a battle we can't win if the Void has a foothold in Valcora."

Ignatius's gaze flicked to her, cold and sharp. "We don't have a choice."

"We could wait for reinforcements," Caspian suggested, his voice calm but edged with doubt. "There are others who would fight with us—if we reach out."

Brea felt a pang of uncertainty. Reinforcements? The idea of calling for help hadn't occurred to her, but Caspian was right—they couldn't face the full might of the Void alone. Were there others in Aetheria that would fight with them?

But Ignatius shook his head. "There's no time. Every moment we wait gives the Void more power. By the time reinforcements arrive, Valcora could already be lost."

Brea tightened her fists, the reality of their situation sinking in. They were heading into the heart of darkness, with no guarantee of success. And yet, despite the fear gnawing at her, she knew she couldn't turn back. The book pulsed faintly in her satchel, a constant reminder of the power she carried—and the responsibility that came with it.

"We need to be smart about this," Lyra said, her voice unusually serious, even for her. "If we're going to have any chance, we can't just charge in blind."

Ignatius's expression hardened. "No one's charging in blind. We'll assess and adapt."

Caspian's gaze shifted toward Brea, his eyes thoughtful. "The Key will be important here. If we can unlock your full potential, it may give us the edge we need."

Brea's stomach twisted. She hadn't fully grasped the extent of her power yet, let alone how to wield it in battle. The thought of relying on something she barely understood made her uneasy.

"I'll do what I can," she said quietly, though doubt lingered in her voice. "But I don't even know what I'm fully capable of. I've barely scratched the surface."

Ignatius's gaze softened slightly as he looked at her, a rare flicker of reassurance in his usually guarded expression. "You'll figure it out. You always do."

His words were simple, but they carried weight, and Brea

felt a strange sense of comfort in them. Ignatius believed in her, even when she wasn't sure she believed in herself.

As they continued their journey, the landscape began to change. The trees thinned, giving way to rocky terrain and rolling hills. The wind picked up, carrying with it the faint scent of the sea from the distant Driftshadow Coast. In the distance, the jagged ruins of Valcora loomed, their ancient stone walls silhouetted against the storm-darkened sky.

"There it is," Caspian said, his voice low as he pointed toward the ruins.

Brea's heart clenched as she looked at the city. Even from this distance, she could sense the power that lay dormant within its crumbling walls. The air around the ruins seemed to shimmer with old magic, a force that had not been fully extinguished even after centuries of abandonment.

But there was something else, too. A darkness lingered over the city, swirling just beneath the surface, a shadow that whispered of the Void's presence.

"We're too late," Lyra muttered under her breath, her eyes narrowing as she surveyed the ruins.

Ignatius was silent for a moment, his gaze fixed on Valcora. "We move stealthily from here," he said, his voice all business now. "We don't want to be spotted until we know what we're dealing with."

You will succeed... Brea hadn't heard that quiet voice in so long, it startled her, causing her to stumble on the path.

Ignatius glanced back at her in concern. "Just sore! I'm

fine." She assured him, not wanting to tell him about the guide's voice she kept hearing.

Her muscles did ache from the long hikes lately, but the adrenaline coursing through her veins kept her alert. The air around them crackled with tension, as if the very earth was waiting for the battle to begin.

They moved forward, their steps silent and cautious as they approached the outskirts of the ruined city. The once-grand walls of Valcora were cracked and crumbling, over-taken by creeping vines and moss. But there was an eerie stillness to the place, as though the city was holding its breath, waiting for something to happen.

Brea's skin prickled with the sensation of being watched. She glanced at Ignatius, who had his hand resting lightly on the hilt of his sword, his eyes scanning the shadows for any sign of movement. Caspian moved ahead of them, his steps careful as he checked for traps or wards.

They reached the edge of the city, crouching behind a fallen pillar that had long since toppled from one of the ancient buildings. Brea peered around the stone, her heart pounding in her chest as she took in the sight before her.

The ruins were crawling with Void creatures. Shadows slithered between the buildings, their red eyes glowing faintly in the dim light. The ground was scorched in places, as though the magic of the Void had seeped into the earth itself, corrupting everything it touched.

"We're definitely too late," Lyra said, her voice low and grim.

Ignatius didn't respond, his eyes fixed on the center of the city where a large, crumbling tower stood. A faint glow pulsed from within the tower, a sickly green light that sent a wave of unease through Brea.

"That's where they're focusing their energy," Caspian said, his voice tight with tension. "They're drawing power from the ancient magic of Valcora. If they succeed…"

Brea didn't need him to finish the sentence. If the Void tapped into the magic of Valcora, they would be unstoppable.

"What's the plan?" Brea asked, her voice trembling slightly. She wasn't sure if it was from fear or the overwhelming pressure of the moment.

Ignatius looked at her, his expression hard but determined. "We stop them before they finish whatever ritual they've started. We take out as many of the Void creatures as we can, and you—" his gaze locked onto Brea's, "—you need to find a way to use your power. If you can disrupt their connection to Valcora's magic, it might be enough to turn the tide."

Brea swallowed hard, the weight of his words settling over her like a stone.

"I'll try," she said, her voice barely above a whisper.

Ignatius nodded, his hand brushing hers for a brief moment before he turned back toward the ruins. "We move in quietly. Stay low. Stay sharp."

Brea took a deep breath, her heart racing as they prepared to enter the ruined city. The shadows of Valcora stretched out before them, filled with danger, with darkness —and with the fate of Aetheria hanging in the balance.

As they moved forward, Brea could feel something pulling her, urging her deeper into the ruins.

The Heart... The guide's voice in her mind urged.

The time had come to face the Void head-on, and there was no turning back.

The battle for Valcora had begun.

CHAPTER NINETEEN
THE BATTLE OF VALCORA

The air in the ruins of Valcora was thick with tension, a palpable weight that pressed down on Brea with every step she took. The ancient city was eerily quiet, save for the occasional whisper of wind through the broken stone archways and the distant, unsettling hiss of Void creatures prowling the shadows. The once-grand buildings loomed around them like skeletal remains of a forgotten age, crumbled and overtaken by time, magic, and the creeping darkness that now threatened everything.

Brea kept close to the others, her heart racing as they moved silently through the narrow streets, sticking to the shadows as much as possible. She could feel the book in her satchel, a steady rhythm that seemed to sync with her heartbeat, its magic tugging at her, guiding her deeper into the ruins.

They crouched behind the remnants of a toppled pillar, peering out at the large tower at the center of the city. A sickly green glow emanated from its highest point, the light flickering and pulsing in time with the dark magic that swirled through the air. The Void had clearly taken hold of the place, and whatever ritual they had begun was already well underway.

"Something's wrong," Brea whispered, her eyes scanning the tower. "The Heart… the book is pulling me toward that place. Like it's connected to something here. I think the Heart is up there."

Ignatius, crouched beside her, glanced at her with a serious expression. "That's where they're focusing their energy. If the book is reacting to it, then the Void is tapping into something old—something that's linked to the Heart of Aetheria's power."

Caspian, kneeling on Brea's other side, nodded grimly. "It seems we've found the Heart, but the Void found it first."

Brea's stomach twisted at the thought. "Then we can't let them finish. We need to find a way to stop it."

Lyra's sharp gaze darted to Brea. "And you're the one holding the key to that." She nodded toward Brea's satchel.

Brea swallowed hard, the weight of their words pressing down on her. She barely understood the full scope of her power, let alone how to use it to disrupt a ritual this massive. But she knew they were right. They had to save the Heart of Aetheria.

"I'll do what I can," Brea said, keeping her voice steady despite the fear gnawing at her. "We need to get closer."

Ignatius's gaze lingered on her for a moment longer, his dark eyes filled with both concern and something else—something unspoken. Then, he nodded, and they began to move again, slipping through the shadows toward the tower.

The closer they got, the stronger the pull of the Heart became. Brea could feel it thrumming in her chest, a steady beat that seemed to resonate with the pulse of the ancient magic swirling through the air. The streets around them grew narrower, the buildings taller, as if the city itself was closing in on them. The stone walls were covered in strange markings—runes and symbols that glowed faintly, pulsing in time with the energy radiating from the tower.

When they finally reached the base of the tower, Brea stopped, her breath catching in her throat. The pull of the Heart was overwhelming now, a physical force that tugged at her, urging her forward.

"There," she whispered, her eyes fixed on a small, half-hidden doorway at the base of the tower. "It's inside."

Ignatius nodded, his expression grim. "That's where they're drawing the magic from. We need to get inside before they complete the ritual."

Lyra and Caspian took up positions near the entrance, their weapons drawn and ready, while Ignatius gestured for Brea to follow him inside. She hesitated for only a moment before stepping through the doorway, the cold stone pressing against her as they moved into the heart of the tower.

The interior of the tower was dimly lit, the walls lined with more of the glowing runes that seemed to hum with power. The air was thick with the scent of ancient magic, a mixture of dust, decay, and something darker—something that set Brea's teeth on edge. She could feel the Heart of Aetheria pulsing against her chest, the power inside it growing stronger with each step she took.

As they descended deeper into the tower, the faint sound of chanting reached her ears. The voices were low and guttural, the language unfamiliar but filled with malice. Brea's pulse quickened as they rounded a corner and entered a large, circular chamber.

At the center of the room stood a massive stone pedestal, and atop it was a glowing crystal—faintly green, just like the light that pulsed from the tower. The Void's magic swirled around it like a dark fog, tendrils of shadow reaching out from the crystal and seeping into the walls of the chamber. A group of hooded figures, their eyes glowing with the same sickly green light, stood around the pedestal, their voices rising in unison as they chanted the ancient words of the ritual.

But it wasn't the crystal that caught Brea's attention. It was what lay beneath it.

Embedded in the stone pedestal, surrounded by intricate runes and markings, was a heart. Its surface was blackened, cracked, and twisted with dark magic, but Brea recognized it immediately. It was the Heart of Aetheria.

Her breath caught in her throat as she realized what the Void was doing. They weren't just tapping into Valcora's ancient magic—they were trying to unlock the Heart of Aetheria's power, to merge it with the Void and unleash its destructive force on the world.

"They're trying to corrupt it," Brea whispered, her voice trembling with shock. "They're trying to use the Heart of Aetheria to fuel their magic."

Ignatius's eyes narrowed as he took in the sight before them. "Then we need to stop them. Now."

Brea stepped forward, her hand moving instinctively to the book in her satchel. The power inside it surged, responding to the presence of its long lost companion. She could feel the connection between the two, the bond that linked them across the ages. And she knew, without a doubt, that if the Void succeeded in corrupting the Heart of Aetheria, all would be lost.

"I have to get closer," Brea said, her voice steady despite the fear gnawing at her.

Ignatius hesitated, his gaze locked on the figures chanting at the pedestal. "It's too dangerous, Brea. You don't know what the Void will do if they sense you're trying to interfere."

Brea met his gaze, her heart pounding. "I have to try."

Before he could stop her, Brea stepped forward, moving toward the pedestal with slow, deliberate steps. The magic in the air crackled around her, the tendrils of dark energy from the Heart reaching out as if sensing her presence. But she didn't stop. She couldn't stop.

As she neared the pedestal, the chanting grew louder, more frantic, and the glowing crystal atop the pedestal pulsed faster, its light flickering as the magic within it began to unravel. Brea could feel the pull of the Heart of Aetheria growing stronger, its power surging in response to the threat.

She stopped just a few feet from the pedestal, her hand hovering over the Heart of Aetheria as she gathered her strength.

"Vathiel en Sareth, revian tul marith!" she whispered, the same ancient words of power from before flowing from her lips as the magic of the book surged through her.

The air around her exploded with light, the power of the Heart cutting through the dark magic that filled the chamber. The chanting faltered, the hooded figures stumbling back as the tendrils of shadow writhed and twisted, recoiling from the light.

With a deafening crack, the crystal atop the pedestal shattered, releasing a wave of pure, unrelenting magic. Brea gasped as the force of it slammed into her, knocking her to the ground. Pain seared through her body as the Heart merged with her.

Through the haze of pain, Brea saw Ignatius rushing toward her, his sword flashing as he cut down the remaining Void creatures. Caspian and Lyra followed close behind, their weapons a blur as they fought to clear the chamber of the Void's influence.

But Brea couldn't focus on them. She couldn't focus on anything but the searing pain that raged through her as the Heart of Aetheria settled itself deep in her chest next to her own beating heart.

"Hold on, Brea!" Ignatius's voice cut through the fog, but it felt distant, far away.

With one final, desperate surge of energy, Brea raised her hand, forcing the magic of the Heart of Aetheria to cut through the Void creatures and end the battle.

The explosion of light was blinding, and for a moment, the world went silent.

And then... everything went...

black...

CHAPTER TWENTY

THE LIGHT AND THE DARK

The light faded, leaving only silence in its wake. Brea lay on the cold stone floor of the chamber, her breath shallow and her body aching from the raw power she had just unleashed. The dark crystal fragments were still pulsing faintly with dying energy. The air around her felt thinner, lighter, as if the oppressive weight of the Void's magic had finally been lifted. But Brea knew better—this was far from over.

She forced herself to sit up, her limbs heavy and weak, and glanced around. The chamber was in ruins, debris scattered everywhere, and the hooded figures that had been performing the ritual were gone, either fled or destroyed in the chaos. Ignatius was at her side in an instant, his hands gently gripping her shoulders, his face etched with concern.

"Brea," he breathed, his voice low, "are you alright?"

She nodded, though the throbbing pain in her chest told her otherwise. "I… I think so."

Ignatius's eyes softened, his thumb brushing lightly against her cheek, wiping away a streak of dirt. "You did it. You stopped the ritual."

Brea blinked, struggling to focus through the haze of exhaustion that clouded her mind. "The Heart… it's inside me."

Ignatius nodded slowly. "The Void's connection to it is broken, for now. But the magic they were trying to tap into —it's still here, still dangerous."

Brea's heart sank. She had hoped that breaking the connection would be the end of it, but deep down, she had known better. The ancient magic of Valcora was too powerful, too deeply embedded in the ruins to be fully destroyed. The Void had only been temporarily thwarted, and the battle was far from over.

Lyra and Caspian approached them, both of them looking worse for wear but alive. Lyra's eyes scanned the wreckage of the chamber before settling on Brea.

"Nice work," Lyra said, though her tone was more matter-of-fact than complimentary. "You bought us time, but this is only a temporary victory. The Void will come back, and next time, they'll be ready."

Caspian, ever the pragmatist, nodded in agreement. "We need to prepare. The Void won't stop until they control all the ancient magic in Aetheria. And now that they've seen the Heart of Aetheria in action, they'll come for it again."

Brea swallowed hard, the weight of their words sinking in. She had barely survived this confrontation, and the thought of facing the Void again—stronger, more prepared—sent a wave of fear through her. But she couldn't let that fear control her. She had to be stronger. They all did.

"We'll be ready," Brea said, her voice steady, though doubt still lingered at the edges of her mind. "We'll find a way to stop them for good."

But even as she said the words, she felt the Heart of Aetheria pulse faintly within her, as if it too was warning her that the road ahead would only grow darker.

Ignatius stood, helping her to her feet, but there was something in his expression that troubled her. His dark eyes wouldn't meet hers.

"We need to move," Lyra interrupted, her eyes scanning the chamber with unease. "The Void knows we're here. They'll regroup, and we don't want to be around when they come back."

Caspian nodded. "Let's go."

Brea took a deep breath, trying to push aside the swirling chaos in her mind. There would be time to process all of this later—if they survived. Right now, they needed to get out of Valcora and regroup.

But as they made their way back through the crumbling ruins, Brea couldn't shake the feeling that something was still wrong. The air felt too still, too quiet. The Void's presence had retreated, but it was far from gone. And then, just as they reached the edge of the city, a low, menacing hum filled the air.

Brea froze, her heart pounding in her chest. "Do you hear that?"

Caspian's hand went to his sword, his eyes narrowing as the sound grew louder. It was a deep, resonant hum, like the earth itself was groaning under the weight of something immense.

Suddenly, the ground beneath them trembled, and Brea's eyes widened in horror as a dark rift split the air in front of them. From the rift poured a swirling mass of shadow, and within the darkness, glowing red eyes blinked open—hundreds of them, staring out at the group with malevolent hunger.

"Get back!" Lyra shouted, drawing her blades as the mass of shadow surged toward them.

Brea stumbled back, her hand reaching instinctively for the book. But as she touched it, the Heart pulsed with a violent, almost angry energy. She could feel its power straining against her, fighting to break free.

"What's happening?" Brea gasped, her fingers tightening around the book as the rift widened, the shadows pouring out faster now, their red eyes gleaming with dark intent.

Ignatius's expression was grim, his sword lowered as the shadows closed in. "The Void isn't done with you yet."

Brea looked at him, confused, just as a figure emerged from the rift. Cloaked in shadow, its form shifted and twisted as it stepped forward, its face hidden behind a dark hood. But there was no mistaking the power that radiated from it—the same power Brea had felt when she first touched the Heart of Aetheria.

The figure lifted the hood of its cloak, revealing a woman who could only be described as the embodiment of cold, calculating power, her beauty a mask for the darkness that festered beneath. Tall and imposing, she exuded an air of imperious authority that demanded submission from all who stood before her. Her silvery white hair, gleamed like the light of a distant, cold moon—untouched by age yet eerily unnatural. Her eyes, a striking, icy blue, seemed to glow with a cruel, almost malevolent light, giving her the gaze of someone who sees far more than she lets on. There was no warmth in them, only a sharp, penetrating coldness that chilled anyone who dared to look too closely. Brea knew those eyes. She quickly stole a glance at Ignatius only to find he still would not meet her gaze.

Seraphina's voice, a soft, deadly whisper, like the hiss of venom slipping through the air, carried across the open space. "You carry the Heart, child, but do not understand the power you hold. Give it to me and I will send you back to your home."

Every word was deliberate, calculated, and meant to manipulate. Brea knew that the woman's calm, quiet demeanor was a facade.

"Who are you?" Brea demanded, trying to keep her voice from revealing how nervous she felt in this woman's presence.

Brea's heart stopped as the woman stepped closer, the woman's cloak disappearing in a wisp of darkness. Brea watched as the woman draped herself in a dark, shimmering gown of black and deep crimson, embroidered with symbols she didn't recognize. A crown forged from obsidian now sat atop her head, its edges sharp and menacing, adorned with dark gemstones that seemed to absorb the light around them rather than reflect it.

"Dear child, don't tell me my son didn't tell you?" The woman pretended to pout, glancing at Ignatius. Brea felt the blood rush from her face. "I'm Seraphina, the Queen of Aetheria. Now, give me the heart!"

And then, quick as a viper, the Queen of Aetheria reached into Brea's chest and pulled.

ABOUT THE AUTHOR

I hope you enjoyed reading this book as much as I enjoyed writing it! A little bit about me: I am a professional nerd who moonlights as a writer, watercolor painter, and football enthusiast. When I am not feverishly Googling obscure facts or creating paintings that could probably pass for modern art (or at least be featured on my mom's fridge), I am busy keeping my book club members on their toes. With a pack of dogs who think they're the real bosses and a love of Alabama football that rivals game-day buffalo chicken dip, my life is a delightful blend of chaos and creativity. Embracing my inner weirdness, I proudly channel it into stories that are just as quirky and offbeat as I am!

www.ingramcontent.com/pod-product-compliance
Lightning Source LLC
Chambersburg PA
CBHW070529160726
48003CB00004B/1737